HOLLYWOOD DREAM MACHINE

Hollywood Dream Machine

A NOVEL BY
BONNIE ZINDEL

Viking Kestrel

VIKING KESTREL
Viking Penguin Inc., 40 West 23rd Street, New York, New York 10010, U.S.A.
Penguin Books Ltd, Harmondsworth, Middlesex, England
Penguin Books Australia Ltd, Ringwood, Victoria, Australia
Penguin Books Canada Limited, 2801 John Street, Markham, Ontario, Canada L3R 1B4
Penguin Books (N.Z.) Ltd, 182–190 Wairau Road, Auckland 10, New Zealand

First Edition
Copyright © 1984 by Bonnie Zindel
All rights reserved
First published in 1984 by Viking Penguin Inc.
Published simultaneously in Canada
Printed in U.S.A.
1   2   3   4   5   88   87   86   85   84

Library of Congress Cataloging in Publication Data
Zindel, Bonnie. Hollywood dream machine.
Summary: Gabrielle and Buffy's long and firm friendship becomes strained
when Gabrielle visits Buffy in California and finds her swept up in a new and
very different life style.
[1. Friendship—Fiction.   2. Self-perception—Fiction.   3. Hollywood (Los
Angeles, Calif.)—Fiction]   I. Title.
PZ7.Z645Ho   1984   [Fic]   84-40257   ISBN 0-670-23220-3

To Paul,
who has taught me what loving is all about

HOLLYWOOD DREAM MACHINE

ONE

MY NAME IS GABRIELLE FULLER, AND ON MY SIXTEENTH BIRTHDAY last summer my best friend, Buffy Byrons, and I opened a bottle of champagne to make a birthday promise to each other.

"I'm going to find love this year," Buffy said, her voice deep and serious, as if she were signing a contract with her own words.

"And I'm going out on my own," I said firmly, almost tasting the idea.

"What do you mean, going out on your own? Do you want to leave home?"

"I'm going out on my own up here," I answered, pointing to my head. "I'm tired of the same routine every day, aren't you? Walking down the same block, passing the same weeping willow tree in front of my house. The same conversations when I open the door. *What'd you do today?* And when I tell them they say,

3

What else? I just want to scream. I don't know about you, but I think there's got to be more out there, beyond Elmont, beyond Long Island, beyond my family."

Buffy stared at me, wide-eyed. "Gabrielle, that's some toast. I'll drink to that," she said. Then, as if the bubbles went *pop* in my head, I twirled the glass around. "I'm going to be *free—*. Watch out, world. *Here I come.*"

We clicked glasses and downed the champagne.

Not many weeks after we made "the toast that changed our life," I started over to Buffy's to make our weekly supply of homemade French vanilla ice cream with an overdose of chocolate chips.

My father was still stuffing papers into his attaché case. "Where are you going this early?" he asked.

"The Byrons."

"Those nut cases? What causes are they into now?"

"What do you mean?"

"What do I mean? Well, there was the time the Byrons marched at the U.N. for Saving the Whales and you girls were up three nights in a row, making Day-Glo picket signs. . . ."

"I didn't mind, I kind of liked it," I said. I guess he felt that was beside the point. So I just went on out the door. " 'Bye, Dad. Don't worry, they don't jump into causes till after ten o'clock."

Buffy's home had something special in it—her mother, whom I called Mom Byrons. When I got there she was sitting at the kitchen table as usual, telling Buffy about an article she had been reading. She dashed over to the pantry to get me some special Danish she had made, then returned to her topic. "The old people have rights but no one cares about them anymore, and the young people, little kids, they have no rights at all.

4

Imagine this three-year-old being beaten by his mother. Look at this picture." She held it up for me to see. I put down the pastry.

"Well, those poor things have no voice," she continued. "I'm going to make a phone call this morning. See what I can do to help." That's what I liked about Mom Byrons, her passionate caring about people she didn't know. I suppose it was at Buffy's house that I got my first glimmer that a world existed outside Elmont.

Mom Byrons put the paper down.

"It's August 15th," she informed us, "Independence Day for India." She pulled out a picture of Gandhi from a stack of magazines she had been saving and lit a few sticks of incense, I suppose to show that she too believed in the peaceful way of living one's life. She had been talking a lot about that lately, since she gave up group therapy and started attending weekly readings on Indian philosophy. She was trying to achieve a more perfect state.

That morning, though, she didn't succeed in even coming near a perfect state. In fact she seemed on edge, the way she darted around the room like a hummingbird. The phone rang and a few minutes later Mom Byrons came into Buffy's room, where we were lying around listening to records. She announced she was meeting Mr. Byrons for lunch and there was some leftover Dijon chicken in the refrigerator. We stayed where we were—it was the coolest place in the house. We didn't even open the door a crack to allow in the scorching heat, until Mom Byrons returned home.

"So you're still in deep freeze," she said, throwing the door open. By the expression on her face we knew there was more than the summer heat to contend with.

5

Buffy and I glanced at each other. We didn't need it in writing to know something terrible was about to happen.

"Did someone die?" Buffy asked.

"No, honey, nothing like that."

"Then what is it?" Buffy demanded, watching her mother.

"We're moving to Los Angeles! Dad was just offered a place in the Economics Department at U.C.L.A., beginning September."

"You're kidding. You've got to be!" Buffy said in shock.

"No, I'm not," she answered, "and Dad wanted to know what I thought. You know how he hates his job at the firm. This will be a chance for him to get back into a stimulating setting where he can teach again. He'd like to do that while there's still time. He believes hope lies with the young people. You know how he feels. Sometimes I think he's a futurist."

All Buffy and I could do was shake our heads in disbelief. "But what about *our* future!"

"Yes, what about us," I chimed in.

By Mom Byrons's expression we could both tell that she had already moved into the future.

Being separated was incomprehensible. Buffy and I spent every day together. When she went to Alaska last summer with her parents the days moved so slowly.

"What about school," Buffy cried out, as the idea slowly started to sink in.

"You'll begin at a new school," Mom Byrons said in a rational voice.

"But what about my junior year at Elmont Memorial?"

"There are schools in California."

Panic was setting in. "Why, that's the other side of the country," I said.

6

"And what about Gabrielle?" Buffy said. "How can we leave each other?"

"Maybe Gabrielle can come visit us," her mother offered. "I know it won't be the same," she continued. "Look, my darlings, don't feel so bad. Nothing is forever, you know. And where is it written that we won't be back here to visit?"

"But what happens in the meantime?" Buffy said. "How will we share everything long distance? You can't share a corned beef sandwich five thousand miles away!"

"Or figure out when the history teacher had a fight with her husband," I added.

"And who'll run home with me in the rain and see which one of us gets the soggiest?" Buffy said, stroking her long chestnut hair like a mane, smoothing it down over her right shoulder. She always did that when she got nervous or upset.

"I hear it doesn't rain very much in California," I said absently. Then my emotions grew uncontrollable, and I burst out, "Buffy, where will I go when I need you?" The thought of Buffy not being there, not sharing every thought, and hope, and fear, was beginning to sink in, becoming more real by the moment. . . . "Oh, I miss you already." My voice quavered and we hugged each other and cried.

"How much is it to call California?" Buffy asked through her tears.

"Well, whatever it is, you'll be able to speak to each other once a week."

"Once a week!" we said in unison. She might as well have said once a year. Buffy and I just sat there across from each other, tears rolling down our faces.

Finally we left Buffy's room because heat wasn't our biggest problem anymore. We thought walking might help, but everything we passed brought back memories, things we had shared since we were five. We passed the brick house on the corner, where we had once believed Russian spies were living. And then there was the mailbox we used as home base for hide and seek. Then we passed the Harris's house, where they left the sprinklers on to keep kids off their precious sidewalk. Everywhere we went, everywhere we looked made us realize that what we had shared for eleven years would soon be coming to an end.

The last week I watched the Byrons pull apart their house. Wardrobe boxes were taped together and labeled. Mom Byrons packed one carton of books after another. We wrapped up the glasses and dishes in stacks of old *New York Times*, put them into big, brown cartons, sealed them with masking tape. And finally all their possessions were taken away by North American Van Lines.

Within a few weeks Buffy and her family had moved to California, and every day on the way to school, I would cross to the other side of the street so I didn't have to pass the "For Sale" sign planted smack in the middle of the lawn. Occasionally a few newspapers were scattered in the driveway, and on the way home from school I would pick them up and stack them in the garage as I always used to do when they were away on vacation. Maybe I thought that, magically, this would bring them back after a few weeks, even though the windows were sealed and the grass was overgrown. I felt like I was in mourning.

I started getting testy at home, mainly because I had no one to talk to. It seemed life was bearable with my parents as long as I had Buffy to complain to about the traumas of each day. I missed Buffy's smile of reassurance.

More than ever, it seemed my parents wanted to know everything. They were looking out for my best interests, they said, but they really thought they owned me. My father wanted to know what time I went to bed, what time I got up, how I spent my allowance. "Get off that phone," he'd shout. "But I'm talking about something important," I'd yell back. And so what if I didn't return my library books on time!

And my mother, well, I didn't want to be like her, either. She used her hands too much when she talked. I'd watch myself do the same thing and get angry. "Am I becoming a carbon copy of my parents?" I worried. I didn't want their life. I didn't want my children having the same teachers I did. I didn't want a house that looked just like the one I grew up in. I didn't want to live on Long Island, have a nine-to-five job, go to the movies every Friday night, and spend Saturday night in shopping malls. Where were the surprises?

With Buffy gone, I felt like the excitement of my life had packed up and gone off with her to California. We wrote incessantly. We'd pretend that we were having one of our usual walking-home conversations, free thought, free association, except now the pen was the medium and all that stood between us were the pages. . . . Months drifted into each other, as letters and the Sunday telephone call linked us.

It was March when I wrote Buffy that no one could ever take her place as my best friend, that my secret thoughts were only shared in my letters to her. And that was about the time Buffy first told me about Zack. I remember the exact words in her letter, "I found this great guy who saves trees and now is working on saving me."

Intriguing, I thought. Certainly provocative. It was hard getting the tone right between the lines; was she suddenly using the helpless-female technique we had used before on Johnny Vacuna, or was she just playing with words? It sounded serious.

I wrote back, "The crop here has been all picked over. Any chance of sending an interesting seedling East? No saps though, we've got our share, as you know. Love, Gabrielle."

The snow thawed, and in its place new green sprouted out in the old willow tree in front of the house. Then one day, about the time the buds opened, I came home from school as usual, and there was a letter in Buffy's handwriting waiting.

Dear Gabrielle,

Are you sitting down? Good. My parents said it was all right to invite you here for the summer. Wouldn't it be great if you could come out right after school and stay through Labor Day? That would give us about 77 days together. I can't wait for you to meet Zack. You'll love him, but I hope not too much! And there's more, more, more to tell but I don't want to burn the post office or the air waves. Just believe me. I'll tell you in person.

Let me know the very second your parents hand down their verdict.

> *Waiting impatiently,*
> *your potential summer*
> *partner in crime,*
> *Buffy*

I held the letter tight in my hand and felt a surge of energy jolt through my body. It was time for me to move my life forward; it was time for *my* adventure to begin! Almost.

10

TWO

TWO OBSTACLES STOOD IN THE WAY OF TOTAL EUPHORIA: MY
parents. Would they let me go? I went to rock concerts in
Madison Square Garden and ice skating with friends at Woll-
man's Rink in Central Park, but there was a difference between
an afternoon's outing in New York and traveling twenty-five
hundred miles!

I heard my mother down in the kitchen, chopping. I think
she was chopping onions, because I heard her start to blow her
nose.

The adrenaline was pumping away as I paced back and forth,
waiting to find courage and go downstairs. Finally, I ran down
the stairs.

When I got to the kitchen my mother was stuffing parmesan

11

cheese into the food processor. She was up to her old Quiche Lorraine dinner again.

"Hi, Mom," I said, ready to explode with my news.

"Buffy had some good news!" she said.

"The *best*."

"Well?" she asked, catching my exuberant mood.

"Buffy wants me to come out and stay with her this summer. Isn't that great!" I hugged her with excitement. From the glimmer in my mother's eyes, I knew she felt my California fever. "Yes," she said, "you two have been separated long enough."

"Then I can *go*?" I begged, my eyes wide with hope. She patted me on the shoulder. "Let's speak to Dad when he comes home."

"But I haven't seen Buffy in nine months," I said, surprising even myself when my voice cracked. "I'll be with her parents. It's not like I'm going off to Europe by myself or anything like that."

All she did was smile. Did that mean yes? Was I winning? Then silence. It must mean no. She must be thinking it over pretty carefully, maybe even seriously considering it. Some wrinkles on Mom's forehead straightened out, and she said thoughtfully, "You know her parents are slightly odd. I mean, I love Georgiana Byrons dearly, she's always been a sweet, giving person. But she's *eccentric*."

"But, Mom, what's the difference if she's eccentric down the block or eccentric in California? Holy cow! You never minded it here."

"Because when she lived down the block, I knew you always came home to me at the end of each day, and I injected some reality. Like the day you saw Mrs. Byrons coming out of the utility closet with the candles burning inside and the smell of

12

incense pouring through the cracks. And you asked her what she was doing in there. And do you remember what she said?"

"Of course I remember."

"What?" she asked, testing my memory or making a point— I wasn't sure.

"She said she was a Ba'hai, practicing all the religions of the world. They're open-minded. There's nothing wrong with that," I said defensively.

She acted as if she didn't hear. "And then you came home asking me if we had a free closet."

"Well, I wouldn't have kept it up long."

"Of course not. We need our closets for our clothes."

"Well, Mom Byrons didn't keep the candles burning very long. She turned it back into a utility room when she joined the Gurdjieff group and went in for group analysis."

"You see? That's just what I mean!"

"See what! What's wrong with being different anyway? Did you ever think that we're the ones who are too close-minded? Did you ever think that maybe we look pretty straight to them?" I asked.

My mother nodded. "Exactly," she said as if winning the point.

She turned around now and looked at me, really looked at me. "Honey," she said, patting my head gently, her tone changing, "I'm not saying no. I'm saying I'll think about it. All right? I know how you feel."

"It's your job as a mother to get me ready for the world, isn't it? I mean, isn't that what mothers are supposed to do? Let me stand on my own two feet."

"I'm just trying to point you in the right direction. That's part of my job, too, like it or not."

13

"Mom, I'm almost seventeen years old. When will you stop telling me what to do? You can't do it forever!"

She tapped the quiche pan on the counter to get rid of the air bubbles and placed it in the oven.

"This quiche. I follow the same recipe but it always comes out different. . . . I'll speak to Dad." I rushed over and hugged her, nearly crushing her ribs, then went off to my room to wait.

I never thought two hours could pass so slowly. But like clockwork the side door opened at the usual time, and I heard my father's voice. Then there was a lot of talk. I tiptoed to the top of the stairs to hear what they were saying, but the sounds were muffled by the dishwasher.

I had to run downstairs. My father was standing there in his pinstripe suit, pulling off his tie and rolling it up. It looked like he had put in a hard day. "Hi, Dad," I said, throwing my arms around him.

My father wasn't one for mincing words, "So Mom tells me Buffy invited you for the summer, huh?"

"Can you believe it! I've never even been to California."

"Don't feel so deprived. I'm forty-nine and I haven't gotten past Boca Raton."

"But, Dad, that's because you never want to go past Boca Raton. You go back to the same hotel every summer for your vacation."

"Well, I don't know, baby. We're talking about three thousand miles. And the whole summer. Let's face it. You've only been away from home for two weeks, and that was when Cousin Connie rented that bungalow up in Lake Placid and brought that drooling dog with her."

"Dad," I said, spreading my arms out into the air. "Look at me," I said. "Just look. I'm as ready as you can get to fly."

14

My mother and father just stared at each other. They were sending these messages across the room to each other like crazy, in the code they had formulated through the years. Their silent conversation finally got the best of me, and I couldn't stand it any longer. "It's not like I'm leaving home and getting married or anything. I'll just be away for two months. What are you so afraid of?"

"Well, if you really want to know," he said, in his paternal, all-knowing voice, "we're afraid of turning your mind over to that crazy family for two months when you're at such an impressionable age, that's number one."

"You mean there's a number two?"

"Number two is we'll miss you, Mom and I. Two months is a long time to be away from home."

"But, Dad, you can't be a human being if you can't live your own life."

I didn't want to get him angry and I could see the color changing in his face. I tried changing my tone, bringing my voice down an octave. "What's good for you isn't always good for me. You're happy staying home, always knowing what to expect. I don't want that. I don't know what I want, but I don't want *that*. I think I'd like not knowing what's going to happen."

My mother and father stood there, speechless.

"Dad," I said, going over and putting my arm on his shoulder. "You wouldn't want a dead fish for a daughter, would you?"

"You're hardly a dead fish," my father answered.

"It's hard to think of you growing up and leaving home," my mother said sadly.

"But I'll be back. It's only two months."

My mother turned to my father. "What do you think, Larry?"

"Why don't we call the Byrons?"

I flew up the stairs, grabbed my telephone book. In a moment I was back down and dialing. My fingers touched the numbers so fast, I set a new record in Touch-Tone dialing. As the number began to ring, I thrust the phone into my dad's hand.

"Hello, Georgiana? Hi, this is Larry. Thanks for inviting Gabrielle out. . . . Yes, of course she wants to go. But first we wanted to know what your plans are for the summer? You're not going off to Alaska to work with the Indians again or anything like that? . . . Nothing like that? You're going to be home all summer?"

My mother's and father's eyes were sending signals back and forth to each other, and I felt like I was watching a Ping-Pong game.

Then my father said the words, the golden words I was waiting for. "*Can she go?*" He paused a moment, then smiled. "Heck, *Sure she can.*" I started jumping up and down and screaming.

The next thing I knew my father was handing me the phone and Buffy's voice came screaming over the other end. "Can you believe it? Can you believe it. . . ?" she repeated deliriously.

"Tell me I'm not dreaming," I shrieked back in a state of euphoria. "What should I bring?"

"First bring yourself, then whatever else. Doesn't much matter. Casual is the word, with a capital 'C.' And I can't wait for you to meet Zack. I told him all about you."

"Zack who?" I asked.

"He's about the greatest person I've ever met," she said.

"You sure I won't be in the way or anything? You know."

"Are you kidding? You're my best friend!"

"And you're mine."

"So what's the problem?" Buffy asked. "You sound funny."

I paused. "Sometimes two into three don't go."

"You're just getting nervous. Zack can't wait to meet you. And who knows? Two into four goes nicely. Zack has a lot of cute friends."

I decided to change the subject before my parents got the drift of romance in the air. "My parents are standing right here now with the calendar. When should I come out?" I asked. My parents were whispering dates and numbers to me at the same time.

"School's out June 15th for me," Buffy said.

"Me, too," I said, circling the date with a red Magic Marker lying there. "That's twenty-eight days," I figured out. "Can't I bring you *anything*?"

"You know what I'd really like? A double corned beef sandwich, lean, with mustard from Saul's Deli. They don't have as good a deli here. And hurry."

"Okay," I said, laughing. "See ya!"

When I hung up I felt like whirling around the room.

"Thank you," I said to my parents. Both of them stood there smiling, like when I had lost my first tooth. And then I knew in a way they were giving me a great gift. A very great gift!

The day before I left, a few of my friends took me for a bon voyage soda at Jahn's Ice Cream Parlour. We ordered the "Kitchen Sink"—eighteen balls of ice cream served in a wash basin—and they gave me a going-away present wrapped in the cover of the April edition of *Silver Screen* magazine. I ripped the paper open, and inside was an autograph book. "Just in case you meet some stars," they said. "And have Buffy sign it, too!"

The last evening, my mother made my favorite dinner, breaded veal cutlet and spaghetti, but I was too nervous to enjoy it.

I was excused from my cleanup duties to finish packing. Most of my clothes were already in the suitcase. I put in my travel clock, a butterfly pin that Buffy gave me the last Christmas, and my favorite junky old Mexican shirt. I was about to close the suitcase when I remembered one more thing—a tiny koala bear that had sat on my bed for twelve years. He was really small and would fit snugly in my suitcase. I felt a little silly, but I used to take him everywhere, so I tucked him down deep where no one would notice him. I heard my mother's footsteps coming up the stairs.

"All finished packing?" she asked, as she stretched out on the other bed in my room. "Are you nervous?"

"Not a bit," I answered too quickly.

"You don't need this junk," she said, jumping up and pulling the old shirt out of my suitcase. Then she disappeared into her room for a moment.

When she returned she had a gold necklace in her hand, her favorite one, with a large gold circle and a tiny deer in the center. Handing it to me, she said, "Take this with you. It goes great with basic white."

"But you love it," I said.

"It can use a change of scenery." She smiled and put it around my neck.

"How does it look?" I asked, admiring it in the mirror.

She nodded her head approvingly, eyes slightly misty. "It looks lovely."

Actually, I thought it looked more sophisticated than I felt and wondered what Buffy would say.

"Do you think Buffy's changed?" I asked.

"Why do you say that?"

"Her voice. It sounded a little different on the phone."

18

"When voices are all squeezed into a little cable it's bound to sound different. Hey, honey, it's okay to be a little afraid."

"I'm not afraid," I answered, taking the necklace off. I knew that mothering voice.

"Of course you're not," she said, smiling. "And after a few minutes it'll be like old times, like you were never apart. . . ."

"I know that."

Then my father came in. He had something in his hand. "Here's a corned beef sandwich for Buffy. I'll leave it in the refrigerator till the morning."

He had something in his pocket, too. "Here's three hundred dollars," he said, counting the crisp, new twenty-dollar bills in front of Mom and me. "Put it in a safe place."

"Thank you, Dad. You're giving me too much, though. I have another hundred dollars of my babysitting money."

"It's better to be safe. Maybe you can buy something special for the Byrons. Now remember what they say, guests and fish have a lot in common. They both stink after three days," my father said, trying to lighten up the mood.

"I'm going to be a perfect guest," I assured him.

We said goodnight, but my mother lingered to give me a special kiss.

"Let's close your suitcase," she suggested, and before I could stop her, she was sitting on the suitcase, pulling on the zipper. Then she put her hand inside to do some quick rearranging, and I know she felt my koala bear. She smiled but didn't say anything.

"Sweet dreams. At least for one more night you're still my little girl."

It was suddenly very quiet. Here I was, going out on my own at last. Why was I feeling scared? I looked around my room.

Was I afraid to leave my parents, leave the security of my four walls? I glanced at myself in the full-length mirror on my closet door.

Would Buffy think I was heavier? More mature? A lot can happen in a year. I kept wondering what lay ahead of me.

I put on my nightgown and got into bed. Somehow I fell asleep. The next thing I knew my mother was standing over me, tapping on my shoulder.

"Wake up, honey. Today's the day," she said. I jumped up, surprised to see the sun shining, grateful that I had managed to sleep at all. I jumped into the shower, then pulled my new dress over my head. There was something exciting about a new dress; it had no history yet. I combed my brown hair and put in two small combs to hold the hair off my face. As we dashed out the door, I grabbed the corned beef sandwich.

At the airport my father hurried us along to the gate. He always needed to be early.

"Do you have your ticket ready?"

"Yes, Dad."

"And your money's safe. . . ?"

"Yes, Dad."

"Don't forget to call this afternoon when you arrive," my mother said.

"I won't."

"And don't forget to write and tell us what you're doing," she added.

The announcement came over the speaker: "American Airlines Flight 23 is now boarding from Gate 40."

"That's you, honey," my father said.

"We still have a few minutes before she has to board," my mother said.

"I better get on." I gave my mother and father a kiss good-bye and hugged them.

"You're on your own now," Dad said.

Almost on my own, I thought to myself, *almost*.

THREE

THE FIVE AND A HALF HOURS WENT BY QUICKLY. FOR THE FIRST half of the trip I read *The Pigman*, and then after lunch they showed a movie. Before I knew it, I heard the loud cranking of the landing gears and the stewardess smiled at me reassuringly. I put on my earphones and listened to the pilot getting his orders from ground control. Some of it sounded like gibberish, and I hoped it made perfect sense to the pilot.

For the benefit of those who believe in seeing everything, they put the landing on closed-circuit TV. In a way I felt protected—nothing could happen to us as long as we were on television. Then the runway opened up before us, the wheels touched the ground, the engines roared into reverse, and I felt solid ground under me once again. Not only was I earthbound but I was alive and earthbound in California.

The plane taxied to the terminal. I edged into the line of passengers, feeling myself breaking out in a sweat. What if the doors jammed and I never got out of here? But the doors finally did open, and I rushed out, my eyes searching the crowd for Buffy.

"Gabrielle. Gabrielle," a voice called out. There she was, weaving her way through the mob. We hugged each other and jumped up and down.

"Let me look at you," Buffy said as we pulled apart. "You look exactly the same, except your hair's longer and you look like a senior now. Tell me about you. What you've been up to."

"I passed all my courses."

"You mean without me?"

"Yep."

"Me, too," she said.

As we headed for my luggage I studied Buffy. Her hair was lighter from the sun, and her skin had a rich bronze tan, but her *eyes*! She had started wearing heavier mascara and brown eye shadow and liner. And her nails were long and manicured. Even her toenails matched perfectly. She never even wore nail polish in New York. As a matter of fact, she used to bite her nails to the quick.

"You look *gorgeous*," I said.

"California is where it's at," she bragged. "You'll think you died and went to heaven. You'll never want to go back to Long Island."

"There's someone I want you to meet," she said, pulling me along. "There he is," she said, pointing to a boy in a red polo shirt and shorts standing near the luggage carousel. He didn't see Buffy or hear her for the moment because he had a Sony Walkman headset on.

"What's he listening to?" I asked, as we got closer, people rushing around us for a good position along the moving rack.

"From his expression, I'd say he's plugged into K-Joy." Buffy smiled. His hair was sandy and continued on into his beard. He didn't see us approaching.

"He looks very intense," I said to Buffy. He was staring at the luggage as it traveled along the conveyor belt. "He looks almost Christlike," I commented.

"Not quite," Buffy laughed, and I had to agree with her that on closer inspection, there was something about his manner that didn't look saintly.

"Gabrielle. This is my man, *Zack*. Zack. This is my best friend, Gabrielle."

"Finally a face to all those stories," he said. So far there was nothing I could hold against him except his being there and interfering with our reunion.

Buffy pulled me off to the other side to wait for my luggage.

"Well, what do you think?" she beamed, waiting for my response.

"Well. He's . . . he's . . ." I stumbled, searching for the right words. "He's taller than I thought."

"He's six feet!"

"You always did like tall guys."

"Yeah."

"And a beard. I like it," I said.

She reached into her canvas pocketbook and pulled out a small present wrapped in shiny purple paper.

"For you," she said, extending it to me.

"For me!" I answered. I shook it. "What could it be?"

"All good things don't have to be six feet," she said, smiling up at Zack. I started untying the ribbon. "Hurry," Buffy said impatiently. "Don't be so neat, rip it off!"

Inside was a silver keyring in the shape of California. Two keys were on it.

"Keys to the house."

"You're kidding!" I laughed, dangling them in the air.

"This way you can come and go."

"But we'll be together, right?" I said. "I really won't need keys."

"Well, if I should be with Zack, and you want to go to McDonald's or something."

"Oh," I said, wondering what she meant. I looked at a saying going around the keyring. "*Mi casa es su casa.*"

"It's Spanish," Buffy said. " 'My house is your house,' and I want you to feel at home."

Buffy saw my suitcase come along and pointed it out to Zack. She knew that suitcase from the times we both threatened to leave home. Buffy and I had packed and unpacked so many times but never put on a mile.

"I'll get the car," Zack said, taking my bag with him.

"I hope I won't be in the way," I said to Buffy, when Zack was out of earshot.

"No, don't be silly." She stared at Zack walking out the double door. "Zack's nice," Buffy said, as if she was trying to explain away a bad cold, "but *you're* still my best friend."

"And you're mine," I echoed.

"I've made some friends, but I don't have a best girlfriend like you. There's no girl here I can talk to the way we did. Girls are different here than they are back East," Buffy said, playing with her hair.

"How?" I asked.

"Sometimes here I talk with a girl and there's nobody home. The conversation is about the weather, moisturizing creams, that kind of thing."

So what if Buffy looked a little different, I told myself. Even though her toes and fingers were color-coordinated and her clothes were more grown-up, underneath was the same old Buffy. I was sure of that.

Outside the terminal Buffy waved energetically. "Zack!" she called, catching his attention. "There was no parking space so he double-parked. He's driving my Rabbit. What do you think of it?" she said proudly. "Actually, my mother and I share it."

"It's beautiful. I love red. And a convertible! I have to share our new Toyota with my mother, too."

"We share everything except the parking tickets." She helped me and my suitcase into the back seat. She jumped in front next to Zack and kissed his neck.

"When I turned seventeen my father said if I didn't get a nose job like I wanted he'd get me and my mother a new car," Buffy explained. She slammed the door and Zack pulled out into traffic. "Take it easy," she said to him. "He said it's got to last a few years."

"But you don't need a nose job," I said.

"Look," Buffy said, turning to the side and giving me her profile. "You know how I always hated this bump. Even in New York. But here, easy come, easy go. If you don't like your nose, you take it off. A girl in my class had her nose and chin done and changed the color of her eyes from gray to blue with contact lenses. No one knew who she was when she came back from Christmas vacation."

"People here are heavy into plastic surgery," Zack said. "They

26

go in to have their faces lifted, boobs lifted, boobs shrunk. One plastic surgeon's wife went to have her feet made smaller to fit into all her old shoes."

"There's so much money here people don't know what to do with it," Buffy added.

"I wonder what that must be like, having so much money," I asked.

"Well, you're in la-la land," Zack answered, as he changed lanes. "You'll see, anything is possible here. You'll find that when you say some girl looks like Brooke Shields, it most likely is."

"God, really!" I said. "It sounds great."

Buffy turned around toward me. "Now tell me what you've been doing and don't leave out a thing." She offered me some taco chips and started munching on some herself.

"Well, not *everything*," I said, pointing to Zack.

"He's very open-minded," Buffy said, socking him affectionately. "Aren't you? Zack's heard everything already. He's into psychology."

"Not my psyche," I answered.

"Zack's going to be a freshman at U.S.C.," Buffy told me proudly.

"That's University of Southern California," he explained. "But actually I'm saving trees for the summer."

"Oh, just for the summer," I said, making a little joke.

"This summer we're replanting two thousand smog-tolerant pine trees." He ignored my comment. "If we don't do this, in twenty-five years smog will have killed most of the trees and nothing would be left except for the barren hills."

"What are they doing for the people?" I asked.

"We plant trees that grow in spite of the smog," Zack an-

27

swered, "and that eventually will help the people."

Buffy patted her chest. "Do you know, when I first came out here I thought I had bronchitis, so my mother took me to the doctor and he told me my chest was clear. What I had was an unproductive cough," she said, banging her chest again.

"An unproductive cough. What's that?" I asked her.

"It's from the smog. It's choking us."

Suddenly I remembered I had something for Buffy. "Guess what I have in here," I said, taking out the brown paper bag and waving it in front of her.

"I can smell it. I can smell it," Buffy said excitedly, opening the bag with the corned beef sandwich. "We better eat it now before my mother sees it," she said, offering me a bite.

"No thanks," I said, "I ate on the plane." For a few minutes the Rabbit smelled like a delicatessen, and it gave me an appetite all over again.

Buffy and Zack devoured the sandwich. "How was that?" she asked, watching his eyes for the answer. "That's as New York as it comes." He smiled and she kissed him. I started twisting the strap of my pocketbook and looked out the window.

We turned off a freeway onto Sunset Boulevard. Every house was landscaped; every lawn looked like green carpet. Palm trees were everywhere and flowers—lilies of the Nile and those exotic orange birds of paradise; it was like driving through one giant florist shop.

"See up there," Buffy said, pointing. "That's Bel Air. A little past that is Beverly Hills. If you've reached that you've reached Nirvana."

I pointed to a white limousine that had stopped next to us at the light. "*Look*," I shouted, "a stretch."

The limousine pulled away before we could really check it

28

out. Between four lights I counted three Rolls-Royces and seven scattered Mercedes.

"Where is everybody?" I asked.

"People don't walk on the residential streets in Beverly Hills," Zack said, matter-of-factly. "They'd get arrested." He curled his beard.

"*Arrested?*"

"Yeah. A few months ago I was walking around the block waiting for Buffy, and you know what? A cop stopped me and asked where I was walking."

"What'd you say?" I asked.

"I said I wasn't walking, I was *waiting*, so they told me not to *wait* like that. Here they shoot first and ask questions later."

I didn't know where his humor ended and truth began.

"He's stretching it a little, Gabrielle. They'll stop and question you."

"Yeah, *then* they shoot." Zack laughed.

"A sick sense of humor, right?" I sat back in the seat and stared out the window, wondering if I would ever feel at home here.

"See that house over there?" Zack pointed. "That's Charles Bronson's house. Some days I see him jogging around the U.C.L.A. campus."

"And Barbra Streisand's main mansion is a mile up the road," Buffy explained, "that's when she's not staying in her Malibu house. And there's U.C.L.A. over there. See that building way in the back " Buffy said, pointing. "That's where my father teaches."

"What a great place to work," I said.

"He *hates* it. He's thinking of quitting and becoming an art dealer. He says art is more stable. It never goes down. Three paintings equal a Rabbit. That's how he paid for the car."

"The country's falling apart," Zack added, in a slightly pompous tone.

"Well, I don't happen to agree," Buffy said, using her debating voice. "I think—"

"It's okay. I think an earthquake'll get us first, so it doesn't matter," Zack interrupted.

"An *earthquake*!" I squealed.

Buffy squeezed Zack's hand tightly. "Doom and gloom, he is! Don't pay any attention to him. Nothing is going to spoil your summer." Buffy extended her hand to me. "Nothing. Not even an earthquake."

Zack made a U-turn in the U.C.L.A. parking lot. "Enough of a mini-tour," he said, taking Sunset to Westwood Boulevard, then making a left turn. And there on the corner near Westwood Boulevard was a lady dressed shabbily in a few sweaters with a shopping cart filled with paper bags. She was sitting on the bus stop bench.

"I guess she's not going anywhere," I said, watching her pick up an old newspaper on the ground, brush it off, and start to read.

"She hasn't gone anywhere for four years. She lives on that bench."

"At least it doesn't get too cold here. In New York they live in the ladies' room or along the subway steps."

The light changed and Zack continued on. Soon we were in a residential area again.

"We're on my street now," Buffy said. "Mom has been straightening the house for days. She'll be glad to see you so now she can stop. I think she missed you almost as much as I did."

Thinking about Mom Byrons made any fears I had vanish. As we drove down the block I noticed a large bush in a leafy lotus shape. "That's my house!" Buffy shouted suddenly.

We pulled into the driveway of a rather humble-looking ranch house. I was relieved at its simplicity.

"Here's your summer digs," Buffy said.

Zack gave me a slightly devilish smile and my eyes darted away. I was waiting for him to say his good-byes and give Buffy and me a chance to be together. Instead he got out of the car and opened the trunk. "I'll bring your bag." He followed us up the steps, where the air smelled sweet; I traced the aroma to gardenia bushes next to the entrance.

"You mean gardenias just grow wild like this in front of your house?"

"They're here for the picking. Everything grows wild here."

"Even us," Zack said.

Buffy just clicked her tongue under her breath and shook her head. "Oh, Zack," she said. Then she bent down, put her hand around the fullest flower, and snapped it off. "For you," she said, handing it to me.

"You shouldn't have picked it just for me," I said, inhaling it.

"That only makes the plant stronger. Another'll grow back in its place."

"Thank you," I said, tucking the flower into my hair.

"Welcome over the threshold," Buffy said, opening the front door.

The scent of flowers followed me into the living room. There was some new furniture mixed with the old I remembered from back on Long Island. I couldn't miss the large new oil paintings on the wall. "Are these all yours?" I asked.

"Daddy's started his collection. He's selling them on consignment. It's part of his transition to becoming an art dealer. He hangs these paintings in the house and brings people around to buy them; he gets a commission and we get Häagen-Dazs sundaes," she explained to me.

The paintings were somewhat surrealistic; the one in front of me showed a head of a man with all sorts of symbolic thoughts floating through his head.

Zack saw my face. "And they're not going like hotcakes," he said. He laughed and Buffy joined in. Obviously they'd shared a few chuckles over the paintings already.

A photograph of a friendly-looking woman with gray hair caught my eye,

"Who's that?"

"That's 'The Mother,' " Buffy said.

" 'The Mother'? Whose mother?" I asked.

"The spiritual Mother. Remember I wrote you that my parents went to an ashram in India? They came back with a Mother, a spiritual Mother. She and her son Shi Orabindo wrote all those books there," she said, pointing to an overloaded bookshelf.

"You mean they meditate and everything?"

"More than that. They have readings here and sell books, too!"

"And your father?" I asked.

She nodded. "They call this the Westwood Ashram."

"Be careful or you'll be next," Zack kidded. "They love to proselytize."

"One mother is more than enough for me," I said. "Buffy, have they got you?"

"Nope. Not yet . . ."

"Does your father believe in 'The Mother,' too?" I asked. Her father had always been more skeptical.

"Oh, yes," Buffy answered. "He was a hard convert, but now he's running the readings, too, and even selling books."

At that moment her father came in, dressed in a blue jogging suit, with a potential customer in tow. He gave me a big hug and hello, and proceeded to show the paintings.

I could see why my father did not see eye-to-eye with Mr. Byrons. They were as different as they come. Although they were equally educated, my father thought Mr. Byrons was an overage hippie, and Mr. Byrons looked down his nose at my father for playing the lottery in the New York *Daily News*.

"Mom, Gabrielle's here!" Buffy screamed upstairs. Mom Byrons came running down the stairs, beaming.

"Oh, Gabrielle. Buffy has talked of nothing else," she said, hugging me tightly. "It's like old times." It was good seeing her again.

"I'm so glad you invited me!" I said.

"You never have to wait to be invited. Can I get you something to drink!" Mom Byrons asked.

"I'd love a soda," I said.

"I'm sorry, I don't keep that poison in the house anymore. It's bad for your system. I have some carrot juice. But no soda."

"Not even Tab?" I said.

"Caffeine," she said, putting her hands around her neck in a choking position. "Let me give you a nice glass of freshly squeezed carrot juice," she offered, with a motherly smile. "You'll like it."

"Sounds great."

It was then that I wished I'd packed some chocolate chip cookies.

"Come on, I'll show you around the place." Buffy led me through the kitchen, which was done in blue tiles with lots of dried flowers and rose petals around. What impressed me most was what looked like twenty bottles of vitamins in a long straw basket. "My mother's trying to get us into healthy foods, but I draw the line at sushi." Then she took me upstairs.

At the top of the stairs we turned left. "This is your room," Buffy said, flattening out a wrinkle on the spread. The room was about the size of my room back home, but that was the only similarity. The large double bed had a brown Indian-design spread on it, and some extra-large throw pillows. "I never had such a big bed," I said, bouncing on the edge. And there was a brass vase with dried flowers on the nightstand.

"My parents bought a lot of this stuff on their trip to India, and when they got home didn't want it anymore, so I got it. I hope you like it."

"It's nice," was all I could say. I wished the room had been basic yellow or some ordinary tone I was used to.

Then she led me to the next room. "And this is Zack's and my room," she said matter-of-factly.

"Zack sleeps here!" I blurted out.

"Only on weekends," Buffy explained. "My mother lets him stay only on weekends, to give me enough space."

The room had a queen-sized bed and there were a lot of dancing figures—the kind that Buffy had always collected, even as a little girl. But before she had collected ballerinas. Now she'd added dancers in pairs. One was a tiny porcelain girl with her arms wrapped around a young man's neck.

"When did you two start sleepovers?" I asked quietly.

"Three months ago," she answered.

"You never mentioned it in all your letters."

"Some things are too personal for letters. I wanted to be with you when I told you."

"Why? So you could pick me off the floor? Well, here I am," I said, my eyes turning away. "Are you ready to pick me up?"

"With Zack out planting with the Tree People during the week, we'll have a lot of time together."

I forced a smile.

"Why don't you unpack," she said, showing me back to my room. "Rest a few minutes, then we'll show you the town. We thought you'd like Santa Monica Pier."

"Who's going?" I asked.

"Zack and I invited another friend. A boy."

"A boy! I'm not ready to meet anyone yet, not even a boy," I said.

"Don't look so worried. It'll be okay," Buffy said reassuringly, patting me on the arm. "I'm going to freshen up," she added, zipping back into her room and closing the door.

I unpacked a few of my things, but I wasn't in the mood so I tried lying down. I was still on New York time, which was three hours ahead of California time. That seemed to be the only thing I *was* ahead in. Then I heard someone come up the stairs and go into Buffy's room. A moment later there was laughter and I recognized Zack's voice. He was in there with Buffy now, and somehow all I felt like doing was calling my mother and telling her that I had arrived safely.

FOUR

WHEN WE WERE YOUNGER, THE THOUGHT OF SEX WITH A BOY absolutely mystified us. What was all the fuss about anyway? In fifth and sixth grades Buffy and I used to sit around for hours talking, trying to understand what was so great about that physical act we'd been voraciously reading about in any book we could get our hands on. Most of the books at her house were nonfiction, and none of them started with the big "S." But when we got hold of a really juicy book, like *Lady Chatterley's Lover*, we would run into the bathroom, lock the door behind us, and sit on the orange shag rug for twenty pages at a time, then put a dot of toothpaste on the page to keep our place till the next time. That's why our books always smelled of Crest.

Buffy had always felt the same way I did about sex. It was something other girls did and we whispered about. Like Doris

36

Hand, the tart of the school. She always wore the tightest sweaters but softened the effect with a little scarf tied around her neck. She would lift her shoulder and twirl the corner of her scarf around her finger coyly. Watching Doris Hand was a spectator sport. Granted I started twirling a few scarves of my own after sixth grade, but no one seemed to notice much. On the other hand, the quantum leaps Buffy was making in this department made me feel that her sexual knowhow could open a gap between us.

Then there was a knock on my door.

"Come in," I yelled.

"Time to get ready for Freddy," Buffy announced, opening the door.

"Who's Freddy?" I asked, peering up from under the covers.

"Zack's friend. Kind of the smart *cowboy* type."

"Does he lasso and do tricks?"

"You'll see," she teased. "Hey, you look all tired out. We can go tomorrow. Are you all right?"

"I'm just hiding."

"Come on out. You don't have to hide." She pulled the covers down off my face. "There you are."

Now Buffy had the old soft smile I remembered on her face, and her cheeks were somewhat rosier than usual.

"You're looking at me funny," Buffy said.

"Am I?"

"Gabrielle," she said, coming toward me. "Is it Zack?"

"It's not Zack," I answered, "it's just that I'm trying to fit all this together and . . . well, you seem a little different."

"I haven't changed that much," Buffy said, sitting on the bed and throwing her arms up in the air for me to take a good look. "But you haven't met anyone yet that you feel this way about.

Wait and see, when you love someone, really love someone, there's no holding back. Like when I knew you were coming for the summer, I rushed to share it with Zack. I want to share everything with him. My thoughts, my feelings, my nightmares."

"Well, I thought we shared everything with each other, too. We're best friends, aren't we?" I couldn't believe the words were actually coming out of my mouth. "Oh, I know what you mean," I added quickly, wanting to retract my last statement. Yet underneath it all I couldn't help but feel that Buffy really was changing. Was it her year in California or was it that some people change more than others between sixteen and seventeen?

It was like she read my thoughts. "I felt so empty when I first moved here. I found myself needing someone, not a best friend, because I have you, but someone different. A boy who needed me, too, and I think I found him in Zack. He makes me happy. He's warm and fulfilling."

"You make it sound like oatmeal," I said. I was sorry I said that the moment the words came out. Sour grapes, I thought.

"Gabrielle, I'm happy with him. Remember those crushes? The Shrimp? The Giraffe? Beef? And now I've finally found someone to love who loves me back. You know how hard that is. And it feels so good. He doesn't expect Miss Perfection and neither do I, and we still like each other. Isn't that amazing? We have our problems, but who doesn't."

"You mean, you're not perfect?" I said with a smile.

"I guess I'm sounding a little freaky."

"No. Just older."

She pulled her long mane over to her right shoulder, then smoothed it down.

"I think you're a little ahead of me," I admitted. "Maybe I need more time to get used to it."

38

Buffy shrugged. "It will happen to you, too, Gabrielle. Somehow it isn't as scary as we imagined."

"It's not?" I said, waiting for more details.

Buffy giggled and gave me an affectionate slap on my arm. "I can't talk about it."

"Did you promise him you wouldn't?"

"If I talk about it, it might spoil it. Besides," she said, her mouth tilting up into a broad smile, "he'd kill me"—and we both broke up laughing.

"What about your mother and father?" I finally had to ask. "Didn't *they* kill you?"

"They are amazingly all right. My mother took me to the doctor for birth control when we first moved out here. She said she'd rather not have me sneak and lie. Here kids live in cars, so she'd rather me be open about it. At least she knows where I am."

"Do you know what my mother would do? I mean, even if it was getting late and I suggested a boy sleep on the couch in the living room for the night?"

"What?"

"She'd grab her keys and drive him home."

The doorbell rang downstairs and I heard a *thump, thump, thump,* like a big orangutan had just been let in.

"That must be Freddy." Buffy jumped up and made a face.

"Come on. Who cares about Freddy! At least we'll be together!" I said.

Zack's voice came booming up the stairs. "Come on! What are you girls doing? Basket weaving?"

"My basket case is downstairs," Buffy yelled, loud enough for Zack to hear. "He likes to be macho in front of his friends."

We started downstairs, but I was in no hurry. I thought about bad blind dates; there had been at least a dozen. One in particular came to mind. He had been two years older than I and worked for his father in an Elmont delicatessen. He didn't come with a bouquet of flowers under his arm; he came with knishes and instructed me to heat them up at 350 degrees for fifteen minutes. That was the beginning of the end.

I finally reached the kitchen. Freddy was standing there. I could tell in an instant that bells would not be ringing. Funny how you can know this in a split second, and I've always been a split-second person.

Freddy reminded me of an owl as he extended his hand. "Nice to meet you," he said.

"Nice to meet you," I said, smiling. Under my breath I wanted to say h-o-o-o-t, as I wiped his handshake off on my shorts.

A dentist had done a lot of work on Freddy's teeth but they still didn't seem to fit.

"So you just arrived this morning from New York?"

"Yes. Have you been there?" I asked.

"Have I been to Fun City, better known as Gun City? Yes."

"It sounds like you've been there and missed the fun," I said.

"Well, at least I didn't get shot."

Zack gulped down his milk. "Let's get moving. The sun waits for no man," he said. Zack and Freddy went out the door, but I held Buffy back.

"Remember our old signal? If I don't want to be left alone with him I rub my left eye? Well, I think it's the left eye all the way on this one."

Buffy threw a jacket in the air to me. "Come on, you're going to love the pier," she said.

FIVE

FREDDY OPENED THE DOOR TO ZACK'S YELLOW RABBIT AND I CLIMBED
in the back seat. I thought his-and-her matching Rabbits seemed
a little like Tweedle-Dee and Tweedle-Dum; at least his wasn't
a convertible. My mind kept playing back that joke about one
rabbit plus one rabbit equals three rabbits. Then I thought, Who
got whose Rabbit first? Did his yellow Rabbit precede hers or
was her red Rabbit first?

"What's so funny?" Freddy asked.

"Nothing. Can't I just smile?"

"You were laughing out loud."

"I was!"

"Didn't you hear it?" His voice rose as he slid in next
to me.

"Hear what?" I said, to annoy him.

"Hear yourself," he said.

"No," I answered.

"Well, we're in the hatch," Zack announced to Buffy as they got into the front seat and slammed the door closed.

An abnormal psychology book, a Dodger jacket, and a crinkled up McDonald's bag were strewn on the floor in the back, on top of a Casio V-Tone musical recorder and an empty chocolate milk container. The carton was turned over, so I picked it up and discovered it held a pretty pathetic seedling. I packed the soil down tightly around the roots. "What's this?" I asked, picking up some dirt that had fallen on the cover of *Seedling News* and putting it back in the container.

"It's chocolate milk," Freddy said. "Soil-packed Chocolate Milk-Delicious."

Looking through the rear mirror, Zack identified it. "That's a baby smog-resistant pine you've got in your hands."

"It's not doing so well back here," I said, straightening it a little. "Do they grow in backseats of cars, too? Are they that hardy? It looks like this one might need some water."

"I brought it home a week ago to plant and forgot to take it in," Zack said, readjusting his mirror.

"Well, maybe we can still save this poor little tree when we get back home," I replied. The wilting leaves had turned brown at the edges.

Zack said, "There's a lot more where that came from. Just throw it off to the side." I put the seedling back down.

Freddy turned on the Casio V-Tone, repeating the same tone over and over. "Nice," he said to Zack. "I have the Casio 500. It's a little bigger." With a large arm motion he put the recorder down then flung his arm around the back of the seat. I moved closer to the window; the knob from the door handle dug into

42

my ribs, but that felt better than Freddy's arm inching down the seat.

We were driving along Wilshire Boulevard and that old lady with her shopping cart was at her bench, rummaging through the garbage. Freddy stuck his head out the window and shouted, "Hey, you want a horseburger?"

"Oh, why don't you leave her alone," I said, winding the window up.

"Hey, you almost caught my nose in it," he said.

"Consider yourself lucky," I said, as Zack made a sharp turn and Freddy fell in my direction. I helped him back to his side.

"Don't worry. When I crashed my last car, my parents said why bother getting it fixed, so they bought me a black Porsche. Right, Zack?" He spoke out over the sound of traffic. "Fit right into the Beverly Hills High parking lot."

"He's got rich parents, Gabrielle," Zack informed me. "On his father's birthday last month he went into Gucci and bought fifteen ties."

"I charged it."

"Fifteen ties," I said. "He can only wear one at a time."

"Yeah, but you don't know which one," Freddy said defensively.

If Buffy had turned around at that moment she would have seen me rubbing my left eye all the way.

Zack turned onto Santa Monica Boulevard now. "I hope we make the sunset," Zack said, as if he had made a date with it.

Buffy pushed down the button that locked her door. "Drive carefully and we might live to see it," she said, giving me a wink. "He drives like a hellion on wheels," she added.

"So you two gals were hatched in the Big Apple," Freddy said, returning to his theme.

43

"Hatched?" I inquired. "You must be confusing me with a turkey. I'm not a turkey. Neither is Buffy," I said.

"God, we're defensive, aren't we? I like New York. I really do," Freddy insisted. "I thought it was great fun trying to hail a cab during the subway strike. My mother saw stars on her last visit to New York when some creep came up from behind and ripped off her gold chain necklace from Tiffany's with one hand and her mink coat with the other. It's a great place to visit, but this is where it's happening."

I wanted to take the psych book my foot was resting on and throw it right at him, but Buffy spoke out: "Right, Freddy. Here they just knock off people eight at a clip at Bob's Big Boy. They go for numbers here." I was happy to see Buffy defending her old hometown.

Zack turned around at the red light. "It's getting so I can't even watch the eleven o'clock news anymore. It's more violent than the movies. It gives me nightmares, hearing all the day's horror just before falling asleep." His remark surprised me, because he didn't strike me as the sensitive type.

"Gabby," Buffy announced from the front seat, "get your first look at the Pacific from the ground." Buffy was the only one in the world who called me Gabby.

"Proof you're on the other side of the country," Zack said, in his matter-of-fact way.

"Wow. It's beautiful," I had to admit, watching the deep blue water framed by swaying palm trees. The cool sea air found its way into my lungs, and I breathed in deeply, holding my breath. It was the first moment I actually felt glad to be in California.

Buffy noticed me. "You can breathe out. There's more where that came from."

Zack turned onto Pacific Coast Highway and we drove parallel to the beach. The sun was setting, streaking the sky with large pink and orange strokes.

"I've never seen such a sunset," I gasped.

"It's the smog." Freddy laughed.

"Oh, shut up," Buffy said. "You're the type who'd run around nursery schools telling four-year-olds that there's no such thing as an Easter Bunny."

"That's all right," I said. "He can't ruin it for me. But you know something weird, Buffy. As we drive along here, those hotels, and the park and everything, I get a feeling of déjà vu, like I've seen it all before."

"You probably have. It's like turning on Channel Two. They're filming down here all the time," Zack said, whizzing by the pier.

"Wasn't that Santa Monica Pier we just passed?" Buffy said, doing a double take.

"I feel like Venice Beach tonight. Is that all right with everyone?"

Buffy looked over to me. "Sure," I said, and Freddy chimed in, "Fine with me. I don't want to make waves."

"Ha. Ha. Ha," Zack answered back.

When we got to Venice Beach Zack parked the car and we walked toward the water. Lots of young people were strolling up and down the beach and the sky had changed to mauves and purples.

"Why don't we rent bikes and ride until dark, then we can go to the pier," Buffy suggested.

"That'll be any minute," Freddy said.

But no one paid attention to him. Buffy and I were great bike riders from way back. We'd ride for hours to Valley Stream State Park and roam around, eat our lunch, and ride home.

"I love bike riding," I said.

Buffy and Zack rented a bicycle built for two.

"Single for me," I told the man, and he gave me an old ten-speed black racer. Freddy started to hop on his bike, but his balance was slightly off. By the time he coordinated his feet and gravity, Buffy, Zack, and I were a block ahead of him.

"Hey, wait for me!" Freddy called out, pedaling faster.

Trendy was a good word to describe Venice Beach. As the sun dropped low behind the ocean horizon, the Venice Beach denizens glistened with a freaky light. Roller skaters, muscle boys, girls with yellow and blue hair—punk queens—were sprinkled among tourists like me. There was also a rarefied collection of windskaters, who breezed by us holding onto colorful red and yellow sails. It looked like fun.

"Excuse me, is that hard to do?" I asked, as one girl sailed right into my bike and nearly fell off her ball bearings. Her T-shirt said SKATEBOARD MAMA. She didn't have time to answer, made a quick recovery, and sailed on by.

All the while I was busy navigating my primitive ten-speed away from Freddy, who was moving in closer.

"Mmmm," I hummed, acting oblivious, picking up speed past a boy riding shirtless. Except for the chain around his waist and the monkey sitting on his shoulder, he looked like anyone else. The monkey was topless, too, except for a pair of sunglasses. These were things you just don't see at Jones Beach.

Pedaling away on the back seat of her bike built for two, Buffy held her hands up and started waving them. "See! *No hands!*" she yelled to me, laughing.

"Me, too," I screamed back, letting go and balancing like we used to through the streets of Elmont.

"*Me*, too," Freddy copied.

"No, Freddy," I yelled out to him.

46

But by the time the words were out, Freddy had his hands waving in the air, and his bike was swaying side to side. Then he came crashing down.

"Ooohhh," he moaned.

We all jumped off our bikes and lifted the bike off while he wormed his way out of the wreckage, astonished to have escaped without a bruise.

"Hey, it's getting too dark. How about returning the bikes?" Zack suggested.

"Okay—on to the pier," Buffy ordered. "I want Gabrielle to see California's version of the Central Park carousel."

"Anything you say," Zack said, giving her a kiss.

"Can't they ever do anything else?" I said under my breath.

A half hour later we were at Santa Monica Pier, and Zack was maneuvering for a parking spot. Lots of cars were there. "Friday night," he explained. We had a long hike through the lot before we reached the white sign: SANTA MONICA PIER.

We walked along the old wooden planks of the pier. Freddy loped ahead with Zack.

"I think I'm having Cosmic Depression," I whispered, and Buffy reached out and took my hand, giving it a good, tight squeeze. "You'll love it out here," she assured me.

Buffy bought tickets for us all to go on the pier carousel. She jumped on a gray horse and I hopped on a white one with a gold mane right next to her. The boys got on the horses behind us, and the carousel began to move. The music picked up speed as we went up and down, faster and faster, and we began to fly past the red plastic clowns and the fake gold calliope tubes. The music grew louder.

Then somewhere in the middle of all that gaudy noise—the weirdos watching and waving and pushing—there in the crowd, near the ticket taker, I saw a boy standing. He was looking at me and his gaze pierced through me. I held on to the reins of the horse. His look seemed to hold me riveted, spellbound. My face felt flushed, and for a moment I thought I would pass out.

"What's the matter?" Buffy called across to me. "Are you okay?"

"Don't worry. I'm okay!"

Now the boy, his light blue shirtsleeves rolled up, was on the other side of the carousel, and it felt like the other side of the world. I thought we would never complete the half turn, but then there he was again. And I wanted him to be looking at me again, too!

He must have noticed my face light up because he smiled at me. If my heart flip-flopped any harder, I'd have had cardiac arrest.

"Gabrielle. Gabrielle," Buffy said. "What are you staring at?"

"Him," I said to Buffy. "Him, with the blue shirt and blue eyes." But this time around there was a girl next to him. Buffy looked and caught on quickly.

"But it looks like he's taken," I said, my heart dropping, the blood rushing out my face. A girl was holding onto his arm as if the wind would blow her away if she loosened her grip. She had blond hair and was very attractive, in a Barbie doll sort of way.

"You never can tell," Buffy said, in a tone I recognized well. "He looks familiar from somewhere."

The carousel slowed down and finally stopped. As we got off our horses I realized Buffy was whispering to me out of the side of her mouth. "Come on. Come on." She winked. "He might hate her. You never know."

I could have kissed Buffy right there and then. Then I saw something that made me think it all must be a dream, because Zack and Freddy had gone ahead on their own and were standing with that boy and talking like old friends who haven't seen each other for a long time. I thought I saw the boy look for me, but I wasn't sure because I couldn't look at him directly. Then Zack said as we drew near, ". . . Brad, this is my girlfriend, Buffy, and her girlfriend from New York."

"Hi," Buffy said nonchalantly. "Yes, my girlfriend Gabrielle Fuller!"

I knew I had to say something but I was afraid he'd hear my heart pounding.

"Hello, Gabrielle." He said my name! Now he knew I existed!

"Hi, Brad," I answered.

"My friends call me Bear," he said, smiling, "And this is Diane," introducing the girl next to him. She wasn't a particularly happy type, I decided, blond hair or no blond hair.

"So you're from New York?" he asked, looking directly into my eyes.

"Yes, this is my first trip here. Actually, *anywhere.*"

"Let's go down to the beach," Zack suggested, pulling his jacket on and zipping it.

Bear glanced over at me. "Great idea."

We all started down the steps to the beach. At that moment, Freddy decided to take a greater interest in me by asking lots of questions: "Do you like beer? Did you ever try smoking a Buddha stick?" But all my attention was on Bear a few yards ahead. He was as attractive from the back as from the front. His shoulders were full, not from weightlifting or anything too extreme, and I could see how he was nicknamed Bear. He looked huggable. And he had a very handsome profile. And his

49

contagious laughter: It wasn't under his breath, or a cautious chuckle; it was a real laugh. Nothing uptight. There was something princely about him. Mostly, though, he seemed so alive.

Freddy by this time was almost doing a soliloquy in my ear, unaware that I had tuned him out. Sand collected in my sandals so I took them off. By this time Freddy ran out of steam and decided to talk with Zack instead. Buffy turned back to me. It was a look of complicity. She was up to something. Next thing I knew, Buffy was striking up a conversation with Diane. Buffy was always good at drawing people out, especially under unusual circumstances.

All I could pick up were snatches of this conversation, like Buffy saying, "Modern dance is just beginning to find a home here in California." Then words flew like "technique," "Martha Graham," "Alvin Ailey," "Twyla Tharp," while Bear dropped back slowly to me. I tried acting naturally, not wanting him to see how much I felt, how much I wanted to *know* him. My cheeks felt warm and I hoped he wouldn't notice.

"Gabrielle. Where'd you get that name?" he asked with a big smile.

"My parents named me after the Archangel. I guess they had high hopes for me."

"I thought Gabriel was a guy."

"Maybe. It didn't matter to my parents."

"Where you from?"

"Long Island."

"That's nice. Then you really don't know many people out here."

"No, I don't."

"Oh. What kind of things do you like to do?"

"I like taking walks. Music. Magic. Things happening."

50

"Maybe we can do some things together," he said quickly, directly, catching me totally off guard. I had heard of "Love for the Asking," but this was ridiculous.

"But . . . what about your girlfriend?"

"Oh, she won't mind."

"I guess we do it differently back on Long Island. A boy usually dates one girl at a time."

"Not here."

"Do you go to the beach a lot?" I asked, trying to keep him with me a few seconds more.

"I like horses," he said. "Did you ever ride a horse on the beach?"

"No," I admitted.

"Then it's a date."

"A date?"

Buffy's conversation could only last so long and Diane turned around to Bear and waited for him to catch up. She also gave him a dirty look. It dawned on me that maybe she was from another place, too. Then we all walked a little bit longer, horsed around, played tug of war with a twelve-foot piece of seaweed until it broke and we tumbled down. I kept watching Bear. A date? When? I wanted to ask. When? Finally it was back to the pier and Bear and Diane were gone. He never told me when.

On the way home I replayed my conversation with Bear at different speeds and prayed he'd find me and call. Buffy told me he knew Zack's phone number, and if he called Zack, Zack would give him her number. Then Freddy interrupted our little whisper session, but now I didn't mind. We were more relaxed with each other, all the tension was gone now that we knew there wasn't going to be anything cooking between us. We even had a few laughs.

When we arrived home the lights were blazing. "Looks like your mother waited up," I said, carrying the pine in the milk carton in.

"No. Those lights are to scare away burglars. Last week someone broke into a house down the block and stole a Betamax and TV. It took thirty-five minutes for the police to come."

"But it's not as bad as New York," Freddy felt compelled to say.

"Oh, shut up, Freddy," Buffy ordered. When we got to the door, Freddy said goodnight and was off. It seemed strange to come home from a double date and have only one boy say goodnight.

Zack went in and turned on the TV, while Buffy pulled me into the kitchen.

"Tell me everything," Buffy insisted, pouring some skimmed milk into a pot, then measuring out four tablespoons of carob, while I watered the little pine and put it on the window ledge above the sink.

"He's wonderful. I can't believe it," I said.

"What did he say?" she asked.

I licked the chocolate-tasting powder off the spoon and sighed. "He asked me out!"

Buffy was thrilled. "When?"

"I don't know. He didn't tell me. Do you think he'll really call?"

"Sure. Zack told me Bear and that girl are fighting all the time. Maybe he's ready for a more mature relationship."

"I hope so," I said, pouring the steaming mixture into three mugs. I'd settle for one even not so mature, I thought to myself. Buffy brought the cup into Zack then turned off the lights and switched on the alarm system.

"Now we're all plugged into the patrol system for the night."

"Well, goodnight," I said, giving Buffy a kiss.

"It's been quite a day," she said. I did a little dance up the stairs. I felt like writing letters back home telling them how terrific California was. I felt beautiful, more beautiful than any beauty shop or plastic surgeon could have made me. I felt so happy I hardly heard Buffy and Zack finally coming upstairs and going into their room.

SIX

THE CALIFORNIA SUN WARMED MY FACE, AS MY EYES OPENED IN AN
unfamiliar room.

Outside my window I heard a torrential shower. Yet the sun
was shining. I ran to the window and pulled open the curtains.
It wasn't a storm at all. It was the automatic sprinkler system.
I gazed out at rolling canyons in the distance, the lush trees and
foliage and the magenta bougainvillea weaving its way up the
low stone fence that surrounded the house. I even saw a hummingbird come toward my window and start feeding from a pink
blossom. It all seemed too good to be true.

I heard Buffy's voice in the hallway, and I opened my door.
"Good morning," I said.

Buffy smiled. "We have one hell of a good connection. Now
we can talk all day without my father screaming you're running

54

up a phone bill, long distance costs money. How'd you sleep?" Buffy asked, tilting her head slightly.

"Great, until the monsoon season hit." I laughed.

"It's timed to go off with the birds," she said.

Her mother heard us. "Good morning, girls, Good morning," she said, giving us each our morning hug. "Time to break your fast," she said, prodding us down the stairs.

The kitchen counter and floor were covered with bags of food. "Did you go shopping already?" I asked, surprised.

"The stores are open around the clock. At six I do my readings, then before everyone else gets up, I food shop. Never any crowds at that hour," she said, starting to unpack.

Buffy helped and I began to put some juices away when her mother put her hand up, stopping us. "No, no, no. You're on vacation. You don't have to do anything but have fun," she said, tying a knot in the plastic bag of greenbeans and putting it in the vegetable bin. "And Buffy can be on vacation with you." Buffy liked that.

"I can help a little," I said, picking up a cantaloupe.

She slapped my hand affectionately. "Enjoy it," she said, smiling. "The summer will go fast enough."

Juice was on the table. "I just squeezed it for the two of you."

"All this vitamin C is going to kill me," I said, slurping it down. "I may never want to leave."

"I always wanted two daughters."

"Want some of this?" Buffy said, holding up a clear plastic bag of something that looked like oats for a horse.

"What is it?" I asked. "Bird food?"

"It's good for you," she said, taking a jar of pumpkin seeds and raw cashews and sprinkling them on top of her cereal. Then she added a spoonful of something else.

"What's that?"

"Bran. Helps your metabolism."

My teeth never worked so hard chewing.

"Where'd you kids go last night?" Mom Byrons asked.

"Venice Beach, then the Santa Monica Pier," Buffy answered. She didn't seem to mind her mother questioning. Whatever Buffy wanted to do, she'd do.

"And you know what happened last night? Gabrielle met someone," Buffy said, her voice turning sing-song.

"She hit it off with Freddy?" her mother asked, surprised.

Buffy laughed. "No, no, not Freddy." We both made a face just thinking about him. "An old friend of Zack's."

"His name is Bear," I almost sang. "Well, really Brad, but his friends call him Bear."

"I never met a Bear before. Will you see him again?" Mom Byrons asked.

I sighed loudly.

"Why don't you invite him over one day?" she suggested.

"For one of the Shi Orabindo readings," Buffy joked, jabbing me in the ribs.

"Well, if he felt the same way, he'll call," Mom said.

"Finished?" Buffy asked, gulping down her milk.

"Ready when you are." I stood up to clear away my own dish but Mom Byrons swiftly removed it from my hands, rinsed it, and had it in the dishwasher before I could ask Buffy, "Where's Zack?"

"He's left for work already. They're replanting a part of Placereta Canyon. A fire burned it out last June."

Within a few minutes we were out in Buffy's red Rabbit, varooming along Sunset Boulevard, seeing more of the sights.

First she showed me the tacky mansion of the Arab sheik who married a waitress from Las Vegas, moved into a four-million-dollar mansion, and then painted pubic hairs on the statues in front of the house. Buffy pointed out that he could spend ten thousand dollars a day without much effort at all. Most of the homes we passed were worth well over a million dollars. "No wonder they say the streets of California are paved with gold," I said.

"There's no place in the world like Beverly Hills. People have too much money here. Some start redecorating their houses as soon as they're finished. Some buy oil wells, for laughs. When they have a sale on Rodeo Drive, that means a five-hundred-dollar dress is reduced to three-fifty."

"Now that's a buy!" We turned off on Roxbury, for my introduction to fantasy land. A Star Lines Tour bus passed, filled with tourists hoping to glimpse a star watering her azaleas.

"I know it's all pretty silly, all of this glamour stuff and people talking about pool motors and root rot, but it's a lot of fun. And it's not hurting anyone as long as you don't take any of it seriously. So, why not?" Buffy said.

Buffy weaved in and out a few streets. "What do you think of that house?" she said, pointing to a large brick house with a tall iron fence around it. Lots of azaleas were in bloom, and the front was dotted with lacy flowers.

"Who lives in there?"

"How would you like to go in one day?"

"Do you know who lives there?"

"*You* do."

"I do?"

"That's Bear's house. Zack gave me the address."

My jaw dropped. "Bear lives in *there*? Are you serious?" I never knew anyone who lived like that. "I guess I'll never meet him now," I said.

"Why not? He lived in that house last night and still liked you, didn't he?" she said.

"Boy, I can pick them!"

"Yep, you sure can! His father's a movie director," Buffy informed me.

My mouth dropped open. "A movie director?"

"Yep," Buffy explained. "King of the 'B' movies."

All the energy in my body seemed to seep away. "Oh, no!" I sighed. "What chance do I have now? We're so different. What would he want with me when he can have all these glamorous girls around?"

"Maybe that's your attraction," Buffy rationalized, "you're not like the other girls." She tapped the steering wheel with her fingers, tapping faster and faster.

"Oh, I don't think I'll ever see him again." I was beginning to feel sorry for myself when Buffy offered her usual words of optimism. "Cheer up, Gabby, I know for a fact you'll see him again. Look. He's getting into his car." I dove under the dashboard not a second too soon, but had just enough time to see Bear walking to a black jeep parked in the driveway.

"My God, he can see us!" I screamed, poking up for another glance. "Get down," I yelled at Buffy. But there was really no way to hide. And no need. The gate opened and Bear pulled out and sped off without glancing our way.

"I wonder where he's going?" Buffy asked.

"Probably to his girlfriend's," I said sadly.

"Naw."

"I feel like we're spying."

"Not really," Buffy laughed.

As we drove I kept thinking about the night before and Bear. I began to daydream about the Western sky and the constellations, and the moon and people traveling there, and Bear!

Throughout Buffy's tour of Bel Air, Muholland Drive, and even the Watts Tower—sights not covered in my father's brochures—all I could think about, all that was on my mind, was Bear. Finally it was time to go home.

As Buffy turned onto her street, it was she who saw it first. There, parked in front of Buffy's house, was the black jeep—with Bear sitting in it—waiting and catching a few rays. He was even more handsome than I remembered. His eyes were the color of the cloudless blue sky.

Bear looked very glad to see us pull up. "Hi, I've been waiting for you," he said, looking directly at me.

"Buffy was showing me the sights," I mumbled.

"I hope she saved some of them for me," he replied.

"I sure did," Buffy yelled as she parked the car.

We got out and headed for the jeep, then Buffy did an abrupt turn and jumped back in her Rabbit. "I'll be back soon. My mother wanted me to pick up her dress at the cleaner's. Yes, lamb chops and the cleaner's!" Before I could yell she got into her car and drove away. Bear and I just smiled at each other.

"She's my best friend," I said, "even long distance."

"Hey, are you doing anything right this minute?" he asked with a sense of urgency.

"No."

"Then let's go for a ride."

"Okay," I said, and jumped into his jeep; I almost hit my head on the roll bar I was so excited. I felt discombobulated by not having to ask my mother's permission or see my father's scrutinizing glance as I said good-bye.

Bear jiggled the gearshift, pushed it into first, and off we went.

"What's *that* gear for?" I asked.

"That's second low. There's lots of hills here. Hey, how do you know about gears?"

"I've driven standard shifts," I said nonchalantly.

"This is my dune buggy," Bear said, tapping the dashboard as if it were a pedigreed Great Dane. "We've put on a lot of miles together. Sometimes I get in and just drive for hours. It helps clear my mind."

"I know what you mean."

"Do you like the beach?" he asked.

"I love it."

"My parents have a beach house in Malibu."

He said it as casually as I would say I have a tape recorder. Where I grew up, one or two families had a cabin in the Catskills; the others would be happy driving from Elmont to Long Beach for a locker at the Capri Beach Club for the summer.

"I love the water but I feel more like an earth person than a sea person," I said, trying desperately to say something interesting.

"Maybe we can change that," he said, smiling. "When's your birthday?"

"July."

"An Independence Day baby?"

"I'm trying. When's yours?" I asked.

"I'm a spring baby. April."

"You walk with a little bounce," I said. I wanted to slap my

60

face for saying something so stupid. Then I knocked off some papers he had on the dashboard and they blew all over the front seat.

I bent down to start picking them up. "There's something else about me you should know," I said.

"What?"

"I don't get along well with inanimate objects; I have these large gestures. Sometimes I even walk into walls. And do you know something that happened once?" I said, placing the papers in a neat pile and putting a book on top of them to hold them down. "Once I slammed a car door on my skirt and continued walking. The skirt stayed there."

"What'd you do?"

"I wrapped the skirt around like a sarong and hoped for the best. And plaids don't wrap well." He started to laugh. "What are you laughing about?"

"It's a riot."

"It *is*?"

"It's nice to see someone who doesn't care about making an impression. Here the girls use Gucci for schoolbags to hold pencils in. Tell me you haven't been Gucci'd yet!"

"Nor Pucci'd."

Maybe Buffy was right: I wasn't like the other girls here. That was what he found interesting, I thought, as the jeep kept bouncing along.

"You're different, too," I decided to say. "Different from most boys, but different in a nice way."

"Really?" He was asking for more.

"I'm not really sure how yet, but I sense it."

"Do you know where I was earlier?" he asked me.

"Where?"

"At Diane's house. The girl you met at the pier. Remember her?"

"Oh." Why is he telling me this, to make me jealous? I wondered.

He stared out at the road, then continued. "I told Diane I didn't want to see her anymore."

"You didn't!" I blurted out before I had a chance to put a cap on my feelings. I hope I didn't sound too happy.

"We haven't been seeing eye to eye on anything. She wasn't adventurous, a real deadhead. Not only that, she was watching my every move. What I did. Where I went. Even my parents stopped doing that to me when I was thirteen."

"I hate it when someone thinks they own me, too," I said empathetically.

"So when I saw you riding that horse I said to myself, Why fight to stay in the same place when there's all that potential out there."

"You said that?"

"Yep, I did . . ."

My feet changed position. "How'd she take it?" I asked.

"She just said okay and went in."

"She didn't fight for you or anything?"

"Nah. We did all our fighting before we broke up."

Between the lines I sensed he must have cared about her very much at one time. They did have a relationship. "Sometimes things end and there's nothing you can do to stop it."

"Are you hungry?" he asked, changing the subject.

"Starved," I lied.

We pulled into the parking lot at McDonald's and went in.

He ordered a quarterpounder with cheese for me and two for himself—plus a milkshake and Tab.

The man placed the cheeseburgers and drinks on the tray. "Here's your chemical shake," Bear said, handing me my order. I just took a few bites of the cheeseburger and sipped guiltily on the "chemical shake." I knew he was talking but I was so self-conscious about chewing in front of him, I didn't hear a word. After he finished eating, he glanced down at his watch. "I have to go to work," he said. "I can take you home, which I don't want to do, or I can take you with me, which I do want to do. What do you say?"

"I'd love to go. *Where?*"

"You'll see."

We jumped back into the jeep and off we went.

"I'll get you home by evening," he said.

"Okay," I said, but I couldn't help thinking Zack must have told him about his "rooming in" relationship with Buffy. I didn't want Bear to think I was shopping for the same.

We passed a gas station and Bear filled up the jeep. There was a pay phone a few yards away. "I'm going to call Buffy and tell her I'll be home later. I don't want her to worry."

"Here's a dime," he said, reaching into his pocket.

"I have one, thanks."

I called Buffy and told her what a day this was. She kept saying "Yippee! Yippee!"—but it felt almost grown-up, almost wonderful, calling and not having to ask someone's permission.

We drove for about twenty minutes before Bear slowed down and made a right turn. I looked up and there was the archway to Twentieth Century-Fox Studios.

"You work here? Are you an actor?"

"No," he laughed, pulling up to the gatehouse guard who waved us on. I tried concealing how thrilled I was being there, but I know the excitement was showing all over my face. But who cared?

"I'm personal assistant to the director," Bear informed me, driving into the studio.

"What does a personal assistant do?" I asked.

"Shout a lot. Tell people what to do. That sort of thing," he said. We drove slowly past a group of painted Indians standing on the grass having coffee.

"I bet you're good at that," I kidded, then continued. "How do you go about finding a job like that?" This definitely offered an alternative to the jobs listed with the school guidance office downstairs at my school.

Bear's face broke into a smile. "Have your father be the director," he said, punctuating the word "father" with pride.

"Don't take this the wrong way, but you sound like a big fan of his," I said.

"To some degree," he said. "He's a wild bird."

We drove onto a cobblestoned street. "There's the East Side of New York, and the 59th Street Bridge, and the railroad." I turned to Bear. "Oh, you didn't have to go to all this trouble to make me feel at home." Then I looked across the street. "And there's Westchester."

"They filmed *Hello, Dolly* here."

"You mean Barbra Streisand sang 'Don't Rain on My Parade' right here on this very spot? I saw the movie four times at the Lynbrook Theater."

"Right here on this very spot." He was enjoying seeing me star-struck.

"But it looks so real."

"That's part of the illusion. That's what people pay for. Want a snowstorm? A sandstorm? A windstorm? What about a trip to the Fiji Islands?"

He caught me staring at some people dressed in silver space clothes crossing the street. A girl dressed in a bathrobe and curlers crossed in front of us.

"See that girl? In a few minutes she's going to turn into a raving beauty."

A man scooted in front of us wheeling a twelve-foot plastic palm tree, while another pushed a large volcano right through the door into the sound stage.

"Welcome to *The Last Volcano*," Bear announced to me.

"This is work?"

"Yep. It's a disaster movie about a group of people in the South Pacific. There's everything in this one: tidal waves, earthquakes. Come on," he said, taking my hand. He led me up a scaffold leading to another scaffold.

"You'll be able to watch from here," he said.

A few people were up on the scaffold already. One woman looked like a reporter, and I was hoping she would talk to me so I could be in a story and my parents would read about me back home. Standing to my left was a weird-looking man who looked like he'd stepped right out of *The Return of the Wolfman*. He had hair all over him and his eyes twitched.

"Make yourself at home," Bear said, pulling over a chair for me.

"I'll try." There were lots of interesting people down below. "Hey, Bear," I whispered in his ear. "Is that what's-his-name, the one who's in *Hill Street Blues*?"

Bear whispered back in my ear. "That's him. He's real trouble on the set. We never know when he's going to show up, or in what condition."

"What about that one over there? I've seen her in a lot of movies."

Bear leaned over again and whispered in my ear. "Her son is a cocaine addict."

"Boy, I'm not going to ask about anybody else. It all looks so glamorous from up here."

Explosions were beginning to go off, and orange and red lights simulated fire in the trees as an active volcano shot red flashes of hot lava in the air. The smell from the gunpowder they were using was beginning to make people cough.

"Home was never like this," I said.

"Now don't go away," he said, holding up his hand, "and don't get too familiar," he said, glancing at the Wolfman. "These lechers love beautiful girls." Then he went down the scaffold. I killed myself for not having my autograph book, and yet I knew I couldn't have asked anyone for an autograph.

My eyes followed Bear as he went. He spoke to a man dressed in a green army fatigue jacket. Then he told someone to move a few palm trees two feet over to the right. It looked funny, watching trees move. Bear went behind the fake volcano that was spewing red-lighted fire, and I found myself worrying about him, laughing at myself for believing it was really a fire. Then the man in the army jacket yelled, "Hey, Bear! Cut one light back there."

I didn't see Bear but heard his voice coming from behind the volcano. "Hey, Dad. How's *that*?" The man responded, "That's perfect."

Dad. That man was his father. I should have known. He was the most dynamic man, moving around lights, volcanoes, people. He was what I thought a movie *mogul* would look like, and an artist, too. His power seemed so enormous. I felt intimidated by his presence, and yet even if he was just like any other father out in front of his house cutting the lawn I would have thought he looked like an interesting man. Then the girl walked onto the set, the one whose hair had been in rollers.

"Okay, let's roll," Bear's father called, and the camera started rolling. A man had to walk across a broken bridge with a child on his back while the volcano erupted around him. The drop was about twenty feet, and all that lay below was a small mattress. In reality the man could have lost his balance and been badly hurt. I had no idea actors took such chances. The actor's face was tense as he walked across, and I breathed a sigh of relief when he reached the other side.

When they finished the shot Bear waved to me to come down and meet his father.

As I came down the stairs, trying hard to be graceful, there was an extra step, and before I knew it, I was falling head first.

Bear came running over. "Are you okay?"

"Fine."

"Dad, I'd like you to meet Gabrielle Fuller."

"How do you do?" I smiled, embarrassed. Why couldn't Bear's father have been an English teacher or something like other kids' dads?

"Well. You *fly* beautifully," he said.

"Thank you. But I really had intended to walk down like everyone else."

"It's more fun to fly," he said, with a warm glimmer in his eye. I could see how people would do whatever he asked. He was magical, and Bear had inherited some of that quality, too, especially around the eyes and cheeks when he smiled. They both had incandescent skin, glowing from within, the kind of glow that makes you wish that a little would rub off on you.

"Are you staying to watch the shooting?" he asked.

Bear answered for me. "Well, she's never seen a film studio before."

"Stay, by all means," he spoke in a full, resonant voice, each word enunciated. Then he extended his arm out like the studio was his. "Show her around." He gave me a penetrating stare, the kind that keeps you there until you're dismissed. Then a sound man called him.

"Excuse me," he said, taking my hand, "I hope I see you again." And he dashed away.

Bear took my hand. "He *likes* you." He seemed pleased.

"Do you really think so?" I asked. Bear shook his head.

"How can you tell?" I asked, searching for approval.

"Because I know my father," he said simply.

Thick cables were all over the ground, and Bear took my arm as we stepped over them. We passed a crew on their break pouring themselves coffee from a giant urn.

"What's it like to have a father like that?" I asked him.

"Pretty good most of the time."

"And the other times?"

"Terrible."

"Terrible! In what way?" I wondered.

"Do you know what it's like living with someone who's famous?"

"No." I shook my head.

"It can be hell," he said, stepping back out into the natural light. My eyes squinted. Then he went on. "You know—to try and be as good as him. It puts a lot of pressure on you. All my life people have come over and said, Your father's terrific, so

68

ingenious, so successful. My father's a great guy, he really is, but how can I ever be all that?" He stopped a moment in his tracks, thinking about what he had just said.

"Who said you had to be a carbon copy of your father? Just be yourself," I said.

"It's not that easy. He's been taking me down to the set or on location with him since I was able to walk. First the nanny came along and then he liked just taking me alone. Like buddies. You know."

"He probably liked sharing it with you. Or maybe showing off his son."

"Maybe. I remember one time on the last day of shooting, I started to cry on the way home. I must have been six years old. I didn't want the picture to end; I believed that the make-believe island really existed and that old native boat maker was real. He was my friend. All of it was real to me, and when they started taking apart the set, banging the hammer through the beautiful backdrop of the island, they were taking it all away. That wasn't a scrim or a backdrop they were smashing; they were smashing my friend's home."

"God, Bear," I said, taking his hand and squeezing it.

"Yeah, and when that reality was over, my father began a new picture, and I began to believe in that one. Finally I learned I could keep trading it for a new one."

"It's a wonder people who make movies aren't all schizophrenics," I said, as we continued walking. I didn't know where we were going; I simply followed him. "Do you sometimes wish your father was a dentist or something? I mean, at least you'd know the office was going to be the same on each visit."

"A dentist's son," he said, giving it some thought. "Never! And be a dental hygienist during the summer?"

We both laughed at the thought. "Then I'd have to say, 'Pass me the cross-cut fishbird drill, please,' " he added.

"Somehow it doesn't suit you," I added.

"No, no, I like all this, I really do. I mean, it's real for me now. The only part that ticks me off is when they compare me to him, my father. I feel like hauling off and socking them in the nose. How can I ever live up to him, really?" It was the first time he showed even the slightest hint of insecurity, and I found his vulnerability attractive.

"Maybe there is a little compliment in there somewhere," I said.

He thought about that a moment, "I think I'll keep him," he said affectionately. "I guess I love him when I don't think I need him so much, if you follow what I'm saying." he said.

"Oh, I know very well," I answered back. If only he knew how well I knew that one.

We came to a golf cart that was parked against one of the buildings. "Step right in," Bear said, holding out his hand.

"Is this my magic coach? Does it turn back into a golf cart at noon?" I asked, sliding in.

"That depends on you," he said, turning on the ignition and pulling away. The motor hummed like a scooter as Bear weaved slightly left, then right.

"Where are we going? Nairobi?" I was getting into the spirit of things. He made a right turn. "Anywhere you'd like," he generously offered.

I was feeling adventurous. "You pick it," I said.

"Good. Then I'll take you home," he said, pulling the golf cart off to the side and turning off the ignition.

"*Home*?"

70

He led me into a dark building filled with old lamps, couches, dummies.

"This is the prop room," he said, throwing a huge bug at me.

"Aaahh!!!" I screamed.

"You don't recognize that cockroach?" he said. "He's starred in many insect movies." We both laughed.

All around the room were large canvases of bridges, buildings, entire neighborhoods.

"It's a little like a rummage sale," I commented.

Behind a bunch of front doors from every period in history, there stood a large reproduction of the Statue of Liberty. "I told you I was taking you home," he said.

"Boy, California has everything, even the Statue of Liberty," I said, laughing.

"Let's go in," Bear said.

"Do you think we can?"

"Let's go." Bear took the lead.

It did resemble the Statue of Liberty, except this model was smaller, and the face wasn't as inviting. The biggest surprise of all was when I walked around to the back and found there wasn't any.

"Where's the rest?"

"That's it."

"How come they didn't finish it?"

"They didn't need to. No one saw the back."

"Why, she got gypped. She's unfinished."

Inside were spiral stairs going up and I followed Bear to the top.

"Here. Take a look out there," he said, pointing out a tiny window near the crown.

I peered out at a panorama view of a world of make-believe. A giant smorgasbord of dreams! And *I was in it*! Then I felt Bear's arm around me.

Staring out at this land of dreams I wondered why I was fighting my parents so hard to let me grow up and lose all this. There was a part of me that wanted to remain a child forever. The only problem was the other part loved being seventeen, and that part of me was next to Bear. Then he did what I knew he would. What I wanted him to do. He pulled me against him and I felt his heart and my own going at a rapid rate.

His smile turned serious, and then his lips touched mine. Now there were no words. No people. Nothing. His lips were soft and relaxed and moved with mine. All my fears dissolved. My fears of being hurt, fears of commitment, even my fears of surrender. My attraction toward him was so strong, all that was left was giving in to it. It was at that moment that I understood why I had really come to California. It came to me as clear as a lightning bolt that struck right into my heart. I was sent here to meet Bear.

It was so *mushy*—but I loved it!

SEVEN

THE NEXT FEW DAYS I COULDN'T GET BEAR OUT OF MY MIND. I REVELED
in the memory of his every word, his every smile. Once or twice
I found myself putting my hand over my mouth, remembering
his kiss. But why hadn't he called? Even Buffy was laughing at
me. "Oh, you're a basket case, all right," she'd say, watching
me loll around the house, drifting off into space. Then we'd
laugh.

"I know," I said. "It feels so good."

Buffy tried to keep me busy. She'd say "a watched telephone
never rings," and then she'd take me for a drive to Westwood,
window shopping. Once I came home with some flowers for
Mom Byrons.

Even Zack tried to help by calling me over when he was
playing Frogger. In one game I got up to the fourth screen

before his alligator got my last frog, just as it was getting safely onto the lily pad. Of course, I had an advantage because Buffy was hugging Zack. He pushed her away. "Hey, I'm concentrating. Leave me alone," he said, just as the game ended and the Frogger song bleeped out.

"Zack and his video games," she complained. "It's a good thing I'm not sensitive." Buffy suggested we leave Zack with his video games for a few hours and snoop around the stores.

"He'll call. He'll call," she said, "but you're driving me crazy waiting." She grabbed her bag and pulled me to the door, shouting to Zack, "Be back in a few hours." He mumbled something back over the sound of Frogger.

As she pushed open the squeaky screen door, she shrieked, "What's this!"

"What's what?"

"This!" She handed me a piece of stone in the shape of a miniature horse. Its smooth body, a marbleized gray, and penetrating eyes had been chiseled with exacting detail; it seemed to have a life of its own.

The saddle was made of brown paper, and in tiny letters, off to the side, was written, as if it were burned in leather, "Gabrielle."

I tore open the note while Buffy admired the carved piece and waited anxiously for the news inside. "Who can this be from?" I asked rhetorically.

"Well, it's not from the Bel Air patrol," she said.

I opened the letter. "It's from Bear."

"Of course, it's from Bear, who else."

My eyes devoured the letter.

Dear Gabrielle,

Since we met at the beach, it seems fitting to return to the beach next time we see each other. Would you like to go to my house in Malibu this Sunday? Autumn Star wants to make your acquaintance. She is my equestrian messenger by day. I made this for you to keep. I hope you like her. Autumn Star is as unique as you are. And I know you two will be instant friends, somehow like we were. I hope your answer will be yes until . . .

Bear

I cradled my horse cautiously in both hands. The brilliant afternoon sun gave the little thoroughbred an iridescence that made it seem to be carved in gold. Buffy was watching my reaction. "What do you think now?" she asked, as if she had written the letter herself.

"I'm speechless." I was deeply affected by his gift. "And it looks like he made it himself," I said. "No one has ever made me a work of art before." I wanted to believe that in some way I was part of his inspiration.

Buffy folded the letter up and replaced it in the saddle. "I think he really likes you," she said.

"Do you know, Buffy," I said in amazement, "this is the closest I've ever gotten to a love letter." Then she smiled, trying to take it out of my hands, but I held on to it. "What are you doing?" I asked.

"I'm just putting it inside for safekeeping. Right here on the piano." She picked up on my reluctance. "Autumn Star won't run away, I promise, at least not until you want her to."

"You mean we're still going?"

"Of course. We can't just sit around here. You can float around Westwood Boulevard. At least we'll get exercise. Anyway, if he cares enough to do all this, believe me he wants to speak to you, too."

"Right," I had the utmost confidence in her ability to crack the code of the male mind.

My day had been made; so had my week, month, and year. She led me to the car and opened the door for me. "It's like I've been dreaming about him all my life and didn't even know it. Now he has a face." I sighed as Buffy slammed the door. I felt myself going off the deep end, but now I could take the plunge because I had more than just hope, or memory. I had a promise of a wonderful afternoon in Malibu.

We parked the car and walked around the stores. Buffy was looking for a yellow striped polo shirt, to match her shorts. Our stomachs began to growl, so we went to Ships. She had a hamburger but I ordered an omelette, so I could make my own toast at the table. Just as the waitress was writing out the check, I saw the old lady with her shopping cart sitting on the bench across the street. She sat there like she was waiting for her bus to come, but I knew she had no place to go. And no one paid much attention to her; they seemed busy with their own thoughts. I paid the check, and as the lady was giving me the change, I asked for a hamburger to go with french fries. Buffy and I crossed Wilshire Boulevard, running quickly as the light changed, clinging to each other as we ran, the brown paper bag in my hand. We sat down on the bench next to that lady. She didn't notice me; she was busy flicking lint off her nubbed sweater. The bus arrived and the people boarded, all except her. Buffy and I went back across Wilshire Boulevard. As the bus pulled away, the old lady noticed the brown bag beside her and picked it up. It was still warm. She felt it with her hands before opening it, then looked surprised to discover a hamburger there, no bite missing. She gobbled it up in a few seconds.

We shopped a few more minutes, but I was getting restless. "Let's call Zack."

"I'm not jealous, I know you're my best friend," Buffy joked.

"Maybe Bear called." My fingers were crossed.

"I know something better, let's go back home. I'll find my shirt another day."

I ran into the house before Buffy even got out of the car. Frogger was still on. I heard the *bleep, bleep, bleep,* when Zack put down the video game for a moment and came to the head of the stairs. "Gabrielle, Bear called," he reported.

"When?" I squealed.

"Oh, about an hour ago. I said you'd be back at four. He'll call then."

Just then the telephone rang, and I ran across the room.

"Go for it!" Zack yelled down the stairs.

"Hello," I said, trying to regain my breath.

"Gabrielle? Is that you?"

"Yes, it's me," I said.

"You seem out of breath. Did I pull you away from something."

"Oh, no. Nothing really," I answered.

"It's me, Bear."

"I know. I know."

"Good. You recognized my voice," he said. "This is the first time we've ever spoken on the phone."

"I knew it was you," I said.

"Good." He seemed relieved. "What are you doing?"

"I'm reading the saddle," I answered.

"Has it hit the big 'G' yet?"

"You mean the garbage? No. I'm going to save it. I never got a letter like that before. And Autumn Star. She's beautiful!"

"Wait till you meet the real one," he said, pleased. "Well, can you go?" His voice wavered, and I detected a slight hint that he wasn't as sure of himself as he had been at our other meetings.

"This Sunday?" I asked.

"Yes."

"I can go."

"Terrific. We can go riding there."

"Riding?"

"On Autumn Star."

Who cares that I'd only ridden once before in my life and that was when I was nine years old. "Love to," I answered him.

"Why don't you ask Buffy if she and Zack want to join us?"

I covered the phone. "Buffy," I called, even though she was only two feet away. "Do you want to go to Malibu on Sunday with Zack?" Buffy paused a moment or two, then yelled back, "Great."

"I heard her," he said. "See you then. I'm at work and someone wants to use the phone." His voice changed slightly, as if someone was listening to his conversation.

"Okay. 'Bye."

" 'Bye."

I waited for him to hang up first, then I almost fell off the chair, "He called!" I said. "He actually called."

"I told you he's crazy about you," Buffy said, hugging me. I jumped all over the place, then turned to Buffy, "But do you know how to ride?" I asked her.

She put one hand on her hips and raised her shoulder and

78

eyebrows at the same time, "Of course not," she said. "I ride just like you." And we broke into a laughing jag that was one of our longest on record.

Then Zack, who had been staring at us all the time said, "It's not *that* funny."

Sunday morning I woke up early. Mom Byrons was having an early morning group reading, so I stayed in my room until I heard all the people arrive and go off into the small garden room on the other side of the house. Then I slipped into the den and put on the Jane Fonda Workout tape, very low. I didn't feel it was sacrilegious or anything that on the other side of the house they were sitting quietly and meditating, while here I was doing jumping jacks. Merely different approaches, I thought, kicking my leg high in the air then rubbing out the pain and switching legs.

By the time I reached twelve situps, I felt a floor vibration by my shoulder. Buffy was standing there counting for me. "One, two, three, four," clapping out the beat. "How's today shaping up?" she asked with a straight face.

I bent over and touched the floor with the palms of my hands, stretching out my back. "Too soon to know," I said in staccato fashion, synchronized to my hands walking out in front of me eight steps, then back.

"Hey," Buffy said, "she's not doing that one."

"I know," I answered. "I'm substituting." She joined me, walking eight counts on the palms of the hands, letting her feet follow. She was good at breathing and exhaled after each movement.

"Zack still sleeping?" I asked.

"Like a bear." She quickly made the distinction. "A grizzly bear." She snorted, then laughed. Then she did a straight split and stretched her stomach toward the floor. Buffy had been the envy of the entire tenth-grade gym class before she moved.

"You are still double-jointed," I said in amazement. "Do you show up your class out here, too?"

Buffy smiled modestly.

"Don't you ever miss home?" I asked, the words spilling out.

She lay on her back and completed a few jackknives with her feet up in the air, "This is my home now."

"Don't you even miss it a little?" I asked, almost hurt.

"Gabby, I didn't leave anyplace, I went to L.A. You know what I'm saying."

"No," I answered. "Not really."

She sat with her back perfectly straight, like a ruler. "It's like another country when you cross the Mississippi, but I'm not where I live. I'm still the same old Buffy inside." The only sounds were our knees pounding against the floor. Then as we stretched our legs out, Buffy turned.

"It's more relaxed, more fun, here," she said. "As long as you don't take it too seriously. You aren't, are you?"

"No," I shook my head, "of course not."

On one hand, as I watched Buffy working out, she did seem like the same old Buffy. But yet I didn't think I was the same old Gabrielle. It's almost that you don't realize how much you've grown until you place yourself back to back with a friend.

"Hey, Gab," Buffy said, as we dusted ourselves off. "You just have to go with the flow." She gave me her best mindless grin.

"But I don't know which way I'm flowing," I answered.

"Even after you got that sweet love letter?" She sounded exactly like her mother.

"A like letter. Not a love letter."

"Okay. A like letter, then."

"Do you want to know something, Buffy. . . ? I think he's the most wonderful person I ever met. Maybe I *am* changing, because I would never have said this before, but I can see myself spending my entire life with him."

She shook her finger at me. "I think you've caught the disease—bad!" she said. "Me, too." She suddenly got serious. Then I noticed Buffy's voice was choked up.

"What's the matter?" I asked her. "Did I say something wrong?"

"No, no, it's not you," Buffy said.

"What is it?" I begged. The air was still. "Are you sick?" I said. She swung open the window and breathed in deeply. When she began to speak, her back turned to me.

"Gabrielle," she said, "I'm pregnant. I'm pregnant and I'm nauseous."

The news shot through me. "You mean you're going to have a baby?" was all I could say.

She played with a small hook on the white shutter, then turned to me. "No, I said I was pregnant; I didn't say I was going to have the baby."

"Does Zack know?" I asked.

She snapped back, "Of course he does. We're making this decision together."

"But you're on the Pill—you told me yourself you went to the doctor."

"Pills are only good if you take them."

I didn't want to offend her, but I was trying to understand.

"You mean you didn't take them?" I was surprised, because Buffy had always been very exacting.

Her eyes darted away from me. "Four days. I forgot. It must have messed up my cycle."

I couldn't help but think how odd it was that I couldn't get an emotional barometer on her. Outwardly she appeared under control, but I couldn't believe that she was so controlled inside.

"I guess I was so relaxed that I forgot to take them."

"But you never forget anything, even shopping lists."

"Well, this wasn't on my shopping list. I don't know how I did it. Ordinarily, I wouldn't let this happen. Maybe in this case I didn't take it seriously enough. Maybe my judgment got a little fouled up."

"Does your mom know anything about this?" I asked her.

"No!" Her answer was emphatic. "And don't tell her, either."

I was surprised. "Why? Aren't you going to? She's so open-minded."

"That's the problem. She'd probably say, 'Great, I can't wait to be a grandmother. I'll hold your hand in the delivery room.' "

In a funny way I *could* hear her mother saying that. What my mother would say, however, would have nothing to do with holding hands.

Buffy's eyes were searching for approval. I smiled reassuringly. "You can make choices, we're out of the Dark Ages, you know. This isn't 1940."

Buffy jumped to her feet, "I have big plans for myself, you know. I want to go to college and study anthropology. And this baby just doesn't fit in with Margaret Mead. And then after that, I still don't know if I want a baby. I mean, who says that marriage and maternity have to go hand in hand? I don't have to have a baby to prove I'm a woman. Not in this day and age. And you, do you want one?" she asked, searching for some kind of validation.

A baby? I asked myself, actually pondering this thought real-istically for the first time. "Yes, I think I do—but not this week."

"Zack and I have talked a lot about it since we found out two weeks ago."

"Two weeks! You were never able to keep a secret from me for two weeks before," I said. My voice sounded surprised, almost jealous at their closeness. Now there was someone else equally if not more important in her life. But in a funny way I was beginning to accept it. "Remember when sex was only something we read about?" I added, in an attempt to take the onus off my last remark.

"Read about? I remember when it was only something we talked about," she said. "I guess I never thought I would get caught like this. Do you think less of me now?"

"Buffy, listen," I said. "I'm your best friend. I'm not just here for the good times."

"But I don't want to bring you into all of this mess."

"Why not? You need me, don't you?"

"Yes, I do. I need you, I really do."

"Good, then I'll be there for you," I said.

"But this is so real," she said, "so . . . so real."

"I know it is," I said, sounding very grown up. Actually, I wasn't quite ready to handle this level of womanhood yet. All these hidden voices I didn't know even existed within me.

"I made an appointment at the clinic in two weeks."

"I'll take you."

"No, thanks, Zack wants to take me."

"Then I'll be there when you get back. You can count on that."

Through all this, I felt closer to Buffy than I had in a long, long time. And I wanted to reach out and soothe away all the hurt and confusion, as we had done for each other through all those years on Long Island.

Mom Byrons had put teal-blue placemats in the sunroom. On the table was a box of natural honey-and-oat cereal next to glass jars of sunflower seeds, almonds, and raisins. As we started mixing our concoction, we heard the group breaking up and leaving through the side door. Mom Byrons bid each person good-bye, then came into the kitchen.

"How are my two girls doing today?" she asked, actually waiting for an answer. That's the way she was, Mom Byrons. She always meant what she said.

"Eat up now. You don't want to be caught without your vitamin C." She squeezed some oranges and poured the juice into glasses. "You're going to need it," she said, pouring herself a cup of herbal tea and sitting down with us. Buffy and I were busy chewing. Mom Byrons watched us for a moment.

"We're going to Malibu when Zack gets up, Mom," Buffy said.

"Terrific!"

"I'd better call my mother and father first," I said, carrying my breakfast dishes to the dishwasher. "I don't want them calling later and wondering where I am. Can I use the phone?"

"You don't have to ask." Mom Byrons smiled.

I started dialing my number. "Are you going to tell them about Bear?" Buffy asked.

"No," I whispered. "They'll get ideas."

I heard my mother say hello. "Mom, hi, it's me." I was surprised at how good it made me feel to hear her voice.

"Hello, darling. Dad's not here right now, he went for bagels.

I know he'll be killing himself that he missed your call," she said.

Other times I would have felt guilty for calling at the wrong time, but I didn't now. Her voice sounded strong, and the connection was so clear that I had to keep reminding myself she wasn't across the street, looking through the window.

"Have you and Buffy done anything interesting this week?" she asked.

There was so much I could have told her!

"Oh, I went to see a movie being made," I said. "At Twentieth Century-Fox. A disaster movie. There were lots of movie stars. You would have died."

"Maybe someday we can do it together," she said. "I'd like that."

"Yes," I answered. "You and Dad have got to come here for a vacation. Now I can show you everything."

She gave me the news from home, and I told her almost everything about Buffy and her house—everything but the living arrangements. Zack came down around this time, his hair disheveled. He headed toward the refrigerator for skim milk. I don't know whether I was afraid she'd hear Zack's voice or his footsteps or what, but one thing I knew, I had to hang up.

"Mom, I've got to go now. It's going to cost a fortune."

"You're worth it," she answered. "What's on the agenda today?" She wasn't quite ready to say good-bye.

"Buffy and I are going to take a ride out to the beach—Malibu. It should be fun," I said, reminding myself I didn't have to ask her permission. I wasn't quite lying, just omitting information. Buffy glanced over at me, smiling at my version of the story, while Mom Byrons yelled out, "Send your mother my love and tell her it's great having you here."

"Did you hear that?" I asked my mother.

"Yes. Give her my love, and Buffy, too. We miss you very much, Dad and I. It's awfully quiet here."

"I miss you too, Mom." I really meant it. "Give a kiss to Dad, and I'll speak to you next Sunday."

" 'Bye, doll," she said. She sent me a kiss, and I sent one back through the wires and cables, all the way back to our kitchen phone on the wall on Long Island.

Buffy got dressed in less time than it took me to pick out my clothes. I put on pants and a soft pink cotton shirt, which made my face look rosy. Then I put on some makeup to help it along. My hair hung loose around my face, California-style. It ended up taking much more time to look casual, and a lot more ingenuity.

Around ten the bell rang downstairs. Mom Byrons answered it.

"My God. He's here, Buffy. He's here!"

"I'm ready," she answered calmly.

I ran down the stairs behind Buffy and Zack. We sounded like a sheriff's posse closing in for the kill. Halfway down, I wished Zack had been waiting downstairs. There was no hiding that he was a boyfriend-in-residence. But there was something about him coming down the steps that telegraphed it—dot, dot, dot, dash. But when I saw Bear's face, all my worries disappeared.

"Hi," Bear said, his eyes looking me up and down.

Mom Byrons shot me an approving glance. He had passed inspection. "Run along now. I'm going to enjoy the quiet," she said. "Have a nice time."

Buffy ran back upstairs and brought down sweaters and handed me mine. "You'll need it when the sun goes down. It gets cool at the beach." Her mother didn't even ask her what time we'd be home. I guess for Buffy and Zack there was nothing that could happen in the wee hours that hadn't already been happening in their room.

"We'll see you tonight," I said to Mom Byrons, setting limits.

The sun was brilliant. "Not a cloud in the sky," I said, walking to Bear's jeep.

"You don't see clouds for months here," Bear said.

"I hate it when the weather is so predictable," Buffy said, like a true New Yorker. "I love it when the sky bursts open and we get sopped." She and Zack climbed into the backseat and I climbed into the front next to Bear. A peel of rubber and we were off.

"Remember when we went out to the beach and got drunk as skunks and started running under the boardwalk?" Zack said to Bear. They both started laughing. "Then we wound up at a 7-Eleven store and he started a fight with a surfer," Zack told us. "The guy and his buddies were about ready to break him in two, so I grabbed him under the arms and pulled him out, screaming, 'My friend is having a heart attack!' "

"Those were the good old days," Bear said, like the crazy times were over.

"We went to Harvard together," Bear told me.

"Harvard in Boston?"

"No, Harvard in Sherman Oaks. It's a private boys' school."

"Very exclusive. You've got to be real smart to get in," Buffy explained. "People start applying their kids when they're born. They say that's where kings are made."

"Buffy and I went to Elmont Memorial High School. It was easy to get in, right, Buffy? They take anyone there. Reverse snobbery."

"How long have you two been friends?" Bear asked me.

"They were in diapers together," Zack answered for us.

"But Buffy got out of diapers first," I added.

When we turned onto Pacific Coast Highway, I noticed a wall along the side. "What's that?" I asked.

"The mountain was falling down. They had to close the road for months," Bear explained.

"Falling down? Just like that?" I asked incredulously.

Zack snapped his fingers. "Just like that." The way he said it, it made me wonder if the Earth was held together with Elmer's Glue. I'd always thought if all else failed, at least you could trust the ground under your own feet.

"Mmm," I said, "so when it seems people are admiring the scenery, they're really checking to see what might be falling on them."

"Right," Buffy agreed. "The Henny-Penny syndrome, we call it. We want to know where the next knock is coming from."

"Exactly," Bear said, moving closer to me. "And see that whole Pacific Ocean down there? All that wet stuff doesn't help a bit if you need water. We had to put a water tank on our ranch. And work nonstop to keep filling it up."

"This place could go up in a minute. Very dry. Lots of sumac," Zack pronounced.

"Let's hope it doesn't." I shuddered.

"Is that the party line from Tree People?" Buffy joked. Zack kissed her for a long time, then they came up for air. "That's the party line," he sighed. I was getting used to all that kissing, but I don't think I could ever get used to all these natural disasters.

Bear turned onto a small dirt road filled with potholes. If the car went a few inches too far to the right, it would be *adios amigos*.

"How do you drive on this road at night?" I asked.

"You hold your breath and pray a lot," he answered. "Especially if you're stoned or drunk. That's the challenge. This is the place," he said, as the jeep approached a wooden fence with a NO TRESPASSING PRIVATE PROPERTY sign. Bear drove right through and pulled up to a yellow-and-white ranch house. A desert garden bordered the driveway with at least thirty kinds of cactus, some flowering. A panoramic view of the ocean stretched beyond the ranch. Two horses grazed in the corral. "They're beautiful," I cried, leaping from the jeep and running toward one of them—I knew Autumn Star immediately. Bear caught up to me.

"Do you like her?" he asked. Autumn Star put her huge head over the fence and let me scratch her nose.

"Like her? Are you kidding!" I said. The other horse nosed in, wanting a few pats, too.

"Autumn Star is an Arabian."

"Hi, Autumn Star," I said, caressing her. A dark pointed star marked her forehead.

Autumn Star didn't move away.

"She likes you," Bear said. "That's her mother over there. Watch out for her. She's possessive." He laughed.

"I know all about mothers," I laughed with him, still stroking Autumn Star's nose.

"Why, she's just a baby," I said, putting my nose to her's. Her hard face rubbed against mine.

"She's two years old."

Buffy and Zack leaned on the fence, waving at the mother, trying to entice her closer.

"We'll ride her later."

"Great!" I said, but suddenly my knees felt a little shaky. Then I noticed a middle-aged man hosing down the patio.

"Carlos!" Bear hailed him. "How are you doing?"

"*Muy bien, gracias. Y usted?*"

"*Fantastico!*"

Half the conversation was lost to me but I could tell they cared about each other a great deal.

"Carlos was at my third birthday." He smiled.

"I wish I had been there, too."

Carlos smiled hello to me as Bear led the way into the house.

It was more rustic than I had expected. A muted, woven rug covered the entire living room, and the furniture, made of bleached natural wood, was the lightest I had ever seen, except for the unfinished kind in a do-it-yourself store. Cactus plants were scattered around, the prickly kind. It was as if we had walked into an indoor desert garden. An enormous succulent had a place of honor near the window. It was nothing like a bungalow in the Catskill Mountains.

I picked a stone out of the mineral collection. "That's magnetite," Bear explained, as he held it up to the light. "I collect minerals wherever I go. My father and I pack our bags and go out for a week at a time hunting for gems."

"Prospect for gold, too?" I asked, intrigued.

"Never turn it down."

I held a glistening stone up to the light.

"That's a piece of gold ore. I found it right here in Placerita Canyon."

"You mean there's still gold in them thar hills?"

"The prospectors left us a few samples. Someday we can go panning for gold. You'd like it."

Zack plopped himself down in the living room and grabbed a guitar that was next to the couch. "Hey, when's lunch?" Zack strummed out in three chords. "I'm starved."

"Me, too," said Bear.

"Coming right up," Buffy said, rubbing her hands together as if she'd run a chuck wagon all her life. The Buffy I knew back home could just about make a BLT. I followed her, the blind leading the blind, into the kitchen.

Buffy pulled some antique-looking vegetables out of the refrigerator. "You be the washer. I'll be the chopper," she said, throwing the head of lettuce to me. "Catch! Hurry, get him. There's a man running to *second*."

I caught the lettuce and held it up.

"He's out," I called.

We rinsed and shredded the lettuce, then mixed in mushrooms, tomatoes, and a can of garbanzo beans we found. Then Buffy cut open some warmed pita bread and put sliced avocado in the center.

"An avocado sandwich?" I asked, placing it on a plate.

"You're in avocado country. You'll love it. Great for the skin."

Bear came into the kitchen and poured beer into large glass goblets.

"Here," he said, handing Buffy and me each a glass. I grabbed mine and licked the foam.

We must have sat around eating and drinking for an hour. Then there was a knock on the door, and the caretaker Carlos peeked in.

"The horses are ready, Mr. Bear," Carlos said.

"Thanks."

"Why don't you two go riding first while Zack and I finish cleaning up," Buffy suggested. "It'll save time." Since there were only two horses, her approach was practical.

"Okay."

Bear grabbed his cowboy hat from a hook in the hallway and took me out on the porch.

"You take Autumn Star," he said, helping me mount the horse on the left side, assuming I really knew how to ride. He stuck the reins in my hands, and I silently prayed lady luck would be riding with me.

The Western saddle felt awkward at first and squeaked as I sank into it. I pulled the reins to the left, and was relieved to see the horse following Bear through the front gates no matter what I did. Bear shifted his weight back as we started down the steep canyon road. I did the same.

Succulents, old pines, and desert flora surrounded us and a scent of leaves and blossoms sweetened the air. We came upon one spot that had its own particular scent. Two wild rosebushes grew there in colors I had never seen before—a faint green and lavender.

"You see this place?" he said. "I don't worry about anything when I come here."

"Do you have a spot like that back home?"

"Yes, Jones Beach. I love to climb out on the jetty and watch the waves break against the rocks," I confessed. "It relaxes me or maybe excites me. Maybe both—that's why I'm drawn to it."

The horses slowly took us closer to the highway, where one of the slopes was particularly steep. I started slipping off but

Bear grabbed my arm and helped me regain my balance. Autumn Star and I continued down the canyon, but as we approached the road she neighed and pulled back.

"Give her a kick," Bear ordered.

I did what he said, and then I saw something moving in the bushes. "A snake!" I screamed.

He rode beside me. "It's only a baby rattler. Lots of rattlers around here."

"Back on Long Island all we've got are worms, and they don't bite!"

Finally we made it to the highway.

"When the traffic clears we'll go," he said, taking hold of the reins close to the bit in Autumn Star's mouth.

"Cars spook her," he explained, leading us across Pacific Coast Highway and onto the beach. There Autumn Star calmed. She inhaled the cool ocean breeze, and her nose twitched. I'd never seen such a beautiful horse before, much less ridden one.

"Let's rest a minute," Bear said, helping me down. He tied the horses to a branch growing out of a cliff, and we sat down on the warm sand. He put his arm around me gently, naturally.

"I have Mediterranean skin. I don't burn easily," I said a little nervously.

He lifted his sleeve up. "See this skin? This is Scandinavian."

"Were your parents from Scandinavia?"

"No. They're both from Beverly Hills. Born and bred here. But I'm one-fourth Scandinavian on my grandfather's side, and it's all here," he said, pointing to his shoulders.

"Actually, I'm all American," I bragged. "I'm very patriotic."

He went to pull me closer to him, but suddenly I felt anxious. I stood up and started petting the horse.

"You really like Autumn Star. I'm getting jealous." He stood up and took my hand, then kissed me on the ear.

I looked away, pretending to be more interested in the topography of the mountains. "The canyons are really beautiful," I said lamely.

"See that line there," he said, pointing out a long burrow in the ground. "That's the San Andreas Fault."

"You mean we're standing on a fault! Why'd you buy a house on a fault?"

"We didn't buy it, we built it. You can't be afraid of those things. Wait—you'll get used to it," he said, kissing my ear again.

"I will? Well, what happens on the day the earth wants to swallow you up?" My breathing was getting heavier.

He laughed. "People have been predicting a major earthquake for a long time now. You kind of accept it as a way of life. I can't be afraid of it, or I'd never be able to get up in the morning."

He reached down and his warm face caressed mine, one side and then the other. Our lips teased each other until we surrendered to the passion that had been building inside. Finally I pulled away. "We'd better stop," I said. "We're on the beach." We untied the horses and started back. The horses quickened their pace, and as we approached the highway again, Autumn Star became skittish. "Pull her reins. Sometimes she thinks she can beat out a car," Bear warned me.

When we got to the other side, the horses started galloping back the way we had come, and miraculously, I didn't fall off. The wind rippled through my hair, and I felt exhilarated by the thrill of it all.

Back at the ranch we filled the buckets with water and watched

94

the horses guzzle it up. They were thirsty, and I was glad to see them drink. Then Carlos started walking them. "Mmmm, I love the smell of horses," I said.

"That's lucky, because we both smell like them," Bear said, laughing.

Buffy and Zack were ready to leave when we returned. I pulled her aside. "Are you really going horseback riding?" I asked.

She whispered back, "Let nature take its course."

Bear started a fire, then held out his hand to me. "Do you want to dance?" He put his arms around my shoulders, and I put mine around his waist. Our feet hardly moved, but his fingers caressed my back in the same slow rhythm. Dancing without music was exciting.

We kept moving around in one place, barely swaying back and forth, until he kissed me again.

I was overwhelmed with emotion, and for some reason a tear ran down my cheek.

"What's wrong?" Bear stopped moving and wiped it away with the side of his hand.

The tear surprised even me. "Nothing," I answered. "I'm just happy."

He pulled me closer to him. "Me, too."

It seemed we weren't alone for more than a half hour when the door crashed open, startling us.

"Those were some horses," Buffy announced, coming in the door with Zack.

"I like the mare. She's hot stuff," Zack said, his eyes very glassy. Bear and I sat on the couch in front of the fire.

Zack turned a record on and nestled his head in Buffy's lap.

"I think I liked our music better," I whispered in Bear's ear. The record had just begun when suddenly the door opened again and Bear's parents were standing there!

Bear kissed his mother hello. "Hi, Dad." He didn't seem thrown by his parents finding us there all cozy. They already knew Zack and Buffy, so the only one he had to introduce was me.

His mother didn't look like a mother at all! She was too beautiful, too glamorous, and yet you could see some wrinkles she was trying to cover up with makeup. Her hair was pulled back off her face, accentuating her high cheekbones and large green eyes.

My eyes were almost the same shade of green as hers, but that's where the similarity ended. She was tall and thin and confident, dressed in white linen pants and a fuschia jacket. She wore gold chains draped around her neck and gold earrings, and diamond rings on her fingers. It was a case of glitter fallout.

"I'm delighted to meet you, Gabrielle," she said.

"Thank you," I mumbled.

I readjusted my blouse, feeling very unglamorous. We all made a little chit-chat, but Zack and Buffy seemed anxious to split.

Finally we said good-bye to his parents, and climbed back in Bear's jeep. When we reached Pacific Coast Highway, Bear turned to me. "Do you want to drive?"

The thought of driving along the coast seemed exciting. "But I left my license at home."

"So what?" he said, giving me the wheel. He jumped over me and stretched his feet out in front of him. "I like to be driven around," he sighed. Little did he know this was the first time I'd driven in California.

It took me ten minutes to feel comfortable with the shift, and another five minutes went by before a police siren came up behind us, signaling me to stop.

"What did I *do*?" I asked, my throat tightening.

"Let's play it by ear," Bear said calmly.

"Tell him I've got food poisoning and you're rushing me to the hospital," Buffy said.

The red lights flashed as I pulled to the side of the road. The policeman got out of the car and headed for me. All I could hear was Zack telling me they shoot first and ask questions second.

"Don't worry, Gabrielle," said Buffy, but I suddenly felt hot.

The policeman peered into the window.

"License and registration, please," he said.

Bear reached into the glove compartment and handed him the registration. My pocketbook was near Bear's feet. My hands shook as I fumbled around for my wallet.

"I left my license at home," I confessed.

"You mean you were driving without a license?" he asked. "Maybe I should escort you home to get it and have a talk with your parents."

"But my parents live in New York," I said.

"Don't they have rules there, too?" he asked me sternly.

"Yes, sir."

"You know I can arrest you and call your parents?" he said in an ominous voice.

I was trembling.

"How old are you?" he asked suspiciously.

"Seventeen."

"I don't know how it is in New York, but you're not allowed to drive in this state without a license."

"I didn't think I'd be driving," I said.

He leaned toward me. "Ignorance is no excuse."

I could see my parents receiving a call in the middle of the night saying that their daughter's in jail and they should come and get her.

"Young lady, I have a good mind to take you in. You kids think you're above the law," he said. Then he heard a call on the radio, and he ran to his car.

"What am I going to do?" I asked desperately.

"We're in this together," Bear answered, his voice cracking a little.

"What are you going to do, go to jail with me?"

Buffy reached over and put her hand on my shoulder. "If you go to jail, I'm going, too. I'll stay with you no matter what," she said.

"Hey, this isn't a pajama party. I don't want to go to jail," I said over the muffled sounds from the police radio. "I don't even want to be brought in." Then the policeman ran back to the jeep, looking preoccupied. "I'll let you go this time, but next time you might not be so lucky. And you get away from the wheel."

He ran back to his car, turned on his siren, and screeched away. Bear came around to the driver's seat, and I slid over. It was then that I felt a long way from home.

A very long way.

EIGHT

DURING THE NEXT WEEKS BEAR AND I WERE INSEPARABLE. AND BUFFY seemed to want Zack's company exclusively. It was like they had made a pact and anyone else would be an intruder until it was all over. After he finished work Bear and I often drove the dune buggy out to his ranch in Malibu, taking long walks along the beach, collecting shells, riding Autumn Star, and talking. But during all the time I never once mentioned anything about Buffy and Zack. It was a secret.

Bear always brought out donuts and beer. First I thought they were for us, but then I noticed he was giving them all to the horses. He said they're crazy about donuts, especially the ones with powdered sugar. So it got to be that on the way to the ranch we'd stop at Winchell's for a box of donuts and a six-pack of beer. When he saw how attached I was getting to Autumn

Star, Bear said I could take her home with me. It sounded tempting but I had to tell him, "My mother made one rule. No horses in the house."

Later we'd drive back into town and go out to eat, stroll along Rodeo Drive, and people-watch. Everyone looked right out of a fashion magazine, and what combinations of colors! Oranges and reds, fuschia and yellow with turquoise.

Most days we were together, he'd call his father. I think he wanted his father to know what he was up to and vice versa. I thought it odd that I couldn't wait to get away from home, while he had all the freedom he wanted and he called his father every day.

Almost a month had passed since we had met on the pier, and I felt ready to tell my parents about Bear. Well, start to, at least. Early Sunday morning Buffy and I planted some tomato plants her mother had bought for us a few days before. And I planted the smog-resistant pine tree, which had been thriving in the milk container. Zack hoed, scooping the dirt up; I planted, patting the dirt down around the stems while I practiced the conversation with my mother.

Then the phone rang. "Telephone for you, Gabrielle," Mom Byrons called in from the kitchen. "Your father's on the phone."

"Hello?" I said.

"Hi, sweetheart," my father's voice bellowed. "What's happening out there? You and Buffy living it up together?"

"Sure we are." I gulped.

Then we chatted a bit. Trivia. Nothing really important. But I had something on my mind.

"Your mother is standing here making hand signals. She can't wait to talk to you. I'll put her on. Here's a big kiss."

100

Then my mother was on the phone. "Hello, Gabrielle. I couldn't wait to tell you something."

"What?"

"I got a job at Hofstra University, assisting the Assistant Dean of Students. You know how I love working with young people. Isn't that great? I start the end of August."

"Great, Mom. And I've got something to tell you, too. I met this great boy named Bear! He's really nice and gorgeous and interesting and different. Like no other boy I've ever met. Ever."

"Sounds like you really like him."

"I do. Maybe he'll visit me next Christmas. You can meet him."

"Gabrielle, sounds serious. How old is he?"

"He's eighteen."

"Bear. That's an unusual name, isn't it?" she asked.

"His real name is Brad," I said, "and he has a great jeep which he calls his dune buggy." Then I decided perhaps I'd said too much. "Don't worry about me, I haven't gone bananas or anything like that." She didn't say anything. "I gotta go now. Buffy and I are off to the beach. Before the traffic builds. Beach traffic, you know."

My mother paused a moment. "I'm happy you found someone special, Gabrielle. I really am. I want this to be the best summer you've ever had."

"Oh, Mom. I hope so. Good-bye now."

" 'Bye," she said, and we hung up. I stood there in shock, my hand still on the receiver.

"What's the matter?" Buffy asked with concern.

"She's happy for me," I said. "Can you believe it? She's happy for me."

"And you didn't even tell her that Bear and you have been going out day and night for weeks."

"Well, I've got to save some of the details for next time," I explained.

Buffy grabbed a granola bar and took a bite. "The way things are going you'll have to talk fast and furious." She laughed. "But don't talk like me."

"I won't," I said. "Hey, aren't you going to give me one?" I pushed my hand into the box for a granola bar. "Ugh! I'm even beginning to like this," I said, chewing away. "Besides," I said, "withholding the truth isn't exactly lying." I shrugged my shoulders. "And I don't want my mother sending the vice squad for what she imagines, or you imagine." I laughed.

"I've never seen you like this before. You're getting so . . . well, so passionate about everything. You used to be calm and low-key." She made me blush a little.

"That's because I've never been in love before. Oh, Buffy, you're absolutely right. What you said the first day I came here. When it happens to me I'll know it. Well, I know it, Buffy. I know it for sure."

"And how would you rate it on a scale of one to ten?"

I paused for a moment to calculate. "A fifteen!"

"Wow, you're hooked," she said.

"I wonder what it must be like to be engaged, that must be a ninety."

"Wait a minute, I'm happy you found somebody, but I don't want to see you going off the deep end and getting engaged or anything," she said.

"Who's going crazy just because I want to feel like a ninety?"

"Sounds like you are to me. You have yourself marrying him already."

She confused me. "I am not," I said defensively.

"Don't plan your life away. Bear isn't a prince. He's terrific, but he's not a prince."

Buffy was letting the air out of the balloon, and I wanted her to stop. "Neither is Zack."

"Hey," she said, putting her arm around me, "I agree with you on that one. Bear is great, he really is. But he's not perfect. I mean, take a look at Zack. He's sloppy, hairy, sometimes he's arrogant and a pain in the butt. But he doesn't expect me to be perfect and I don't expect perfection from him either. You can see that. So we get along just fine. At least in that way there's hope for us. We're not laying a trip on each other. So all I'm saying is try and see Bear as he really is. I think he's awfully nice."

Buffy waited for me to say something, but I didn't. I sat there thinking about what she was saying. Then Buffy filled the gap. "I know I don't want to be anybody's dream girl and I'm sure you don't want to be either. It's too hard. And you can never win. You can't."

On Monday Bear arrived early; he had the morning off and we were spending it together. Buffy was waiting for Zack to finish his grafting workshop and then they were going out. Today was her clinic appointment, and I knew that's why she was nervous.

"Come on, girl," Bear said, pulling me off the chair. "We're not going as far as the mountains today; we're going to my house in town. Maybe play some tennis or something." I didn't have the heart or courage to say how little I knew about playing tennis or how I would be watching the clock for Buffy's appointment. "I just have to be home by three."

"What happens, do you turn into a pumpkin?" he asked,

taking my hand. "Just don't disappear on me," he added as we left the house.

He feels the same way I do, I thought as we got into his jeep.

As Bear turned off at Benedict Canyon and pulled up to the impressive black gate, I laughed under my breath, remembering me ducking under the dashboard of Buffy's car so as not to get caught spying in front of Bear's house.

"What's so funny?" he asked. The automatic gate opened.

"Nothing," I said, as he pulled up to this mansion he called home. His house had seemed immense from the outside, but it looked even bigger as we pulled around the circular drive. The black shutters against the stately old brick, the burst of flowers in bloom, and the perfectly manicured lawn with palm trees glistening in the sun gave his home a sense of drama.

He pulled his jeep up between a white Rolls-Royce and a two-seater Mercedes-Benz, and we went inside.

The hallway chandelier turned incandescent as sunshine struck the crystals. I saw fresh floral arrangements everywhere and the dark wood floor smelled freshly polished. A housekeeper was vacuuming in her starched white uniform. Bear led me past an antique credenza into the kitchen, where a huge oil painting hung. It was the first time I'd ever seen a painting, an original oil painting, in a kitchen. Not even at Buffy's house. I remembered Buffy's instructions: Don't take it all seriously; enjoy it.

Bear's mother came into the kitchen, looking as glamorous as the first time we met. Today she wore a summer dress and beads which looked more youthful than her years. It made me wonder how old she really was.

"Mom, you remember Gabrielle," he said.

"Of course. I was just sitting down for a cup of coffee. Want to join me?" she asked.

She started to pour herself a cup of coffee from a white ceramic coffee pot, but the maid in the starched white uniform stopped her. "Sit down, Miss Dora, I'll get it for you," she said.

"Make it two, please," she instructed, pulling out a chair for me to sit next to her.

"Thank you, Mrs. Randolph." I did as she instructed.

Then she pulled out swatches of fabric. "Which do you like better, the L'Etoile pattern or the green floral motif?"

"The L'Etoile," I answered, "because I like saying the word 'L'Etoile' better."

"It's for the living room sofa." The L'Etoile swatch got placed on one side of the table as she considered it seriously.

"With the heavy rains last March some water leaked in. The flood insurance will take care of it."

"You get flood insurance?" I asked.

"Oh, yes. Earthquake insurance, too. Come with me," she said suddenly. She led me down the three steps into her sunken living room and pointed out the sofa she was referring to. The only thought that ran through my mind was how long my parents had saved to buy their new sofa and it looked a lot worse than this one.

"Don't you think a blue sofa?" she asked.

"Definitely blue."

"It needs a little sprucing up in here," she said, spinning around the room. "See all this, it got wet; water seeped in and buckled the print," she said, straightening out a picture frame on the wall. "It's a signed lithograph." It had a number on the bottom and a signature I couldn't read. "And this picture that Brad did," she said, pointing it out. "It's going."

"Going where?" I asked.

"Out."

"Out?"

"There's nothing that can't be replaced," she said matter-of-factly.

"But Bear's picture."

"Oh, he'll do another."

"Oh," I said, not really understanding.

"Actually, insurance-wise it was a very successful flood."

Just then a buzzer went off and she rushed back to the kitchen, pushed a few buttons on the microwave, reset the timer, and came back to finish her coffee. Before she had a chance to sit down, another buzzer, this one two tones higher, buzzed. She got up and pushed a red button on the wall.

"The gate. Must be the pool man," she explained, turning to her seat. "All this buzzing is giving me a headache."

Boy, I thought, I wouldn't complain about pushing a buzzer and having my pool cleaned for me. I wouldn't mind a headache over this. She went on to tell me about an auction she was going to on Saturday where they'd be selling Ming dynasty art. She didn't much like it, but it was worth a fortune. Bear put down his empty juice glass and paced the terra-cotta tile floor, bouncing the tennis ball on his racket. "You two can talk later," he said at last, opening the door and leading me out.

He led me onto the sparkling tennis court and handed me his mother's aluminum tennis racket. "This should be the right weight for you," he said. It felt much lighter than I expected, not that that would make any difference. Then he nestled up behind me. "Let me see your grip." I demonstrated my grip.

"At least you haven't picked up any bad habits." He came around the net and demonstrated how to follow through on the ball. "Swing as if you're caressing the racket," he said, sliding his hand over my hand. "Follow through." We hit a few balls. "Good." He seemed pleased. "You're doing better."

"Then how come all the yellow balls are on my side?"

"They don't call me Tennis the Menace for nothing. Look— the key is to relax."

"Relax. How?" I asked.

"Stop worrying, for one thing," he said, shading the sun from his eyes.

"I'll try," I said, but it wasn't that easy.

We hit the ball back and forth until the midday sun started to bake us. Beads of perspiration were forming on my forehead.

"That's enough for today," Bear said, wiping his face on his sleeve, then going to the water cooler in a gazebo near the court. He handed me a cup of purified water. "Have I exhausted you already?" he asked, gulping down his cup of water. "Come on. Let's go for a swim."

"It's like a resort here," I said, smiling. "New York was never like this." When I took my watch off, I saw it was one o'clock. Buffy must be at the clinic by now.

A few bathing suits were hanging on fish-shaped hooks in the white cabana. Bear told me to pick any one that fit. A white suit with red trim fit perfectly. I checked myself in the full-length mirror, patted my stomach in, and followed Bear with a running jump into the kidney-shaped pool. The bottom of the pool was painted black, and little blue-and-white plastic dolphins were bobbing around everywhere.

Every pool I had ever been in was filled with people, mostly strangers. Here in this huge pool there were just the two of us. I felt so elite. Bear swam to the side of the pool and held on to the edge. I swam over to him and he put his arms around me, looking very serious. I could tell there was something on his mind.

"My father asked me to go to Santa Barbara, check out possible location sites for his next picture."

"When do you have to go?" I asked, suddenly cold.

"Next Friday. Just overnight."

"Oh," I said, relieved.

"But what I wanted to ask you was if you wanted to go with me."

"You mean stay there overnight?" I asked.

"Yes," Bear answered. "It's not that far away; two hours, but it's a great place."

It could just as well have been five minutes away. I didn't say a word.

"Well, what do you think?" he asked, waiting for an answer.

"I don't know," I answered slowly.

"We can be together, just *us*," he said, smiling. Silence. "Don't you want to be with me?"

Suddenly my thoughts became surprisingly clear. "Of course I want to be with you, but that's not the point." That didn't come out right. "I don't know that I'm ready to go away with you like that."

He trickled some water over his fingers. "I thought you cared about me." His expression was half pouting.

"I do care about you. Let me think about it, okay?"

He threw some water over his chest. "Gabrielle, I'm not going to push you, but sometimes a person can think about something too much and think themselves right out of doing what they want to do. But I'm not going to push." He did a nosedive into the bottom of the pool and swam the entire length before surfacing. As I watched him swim back and forth I thought how

108

lovely it would be to wake up in his arms in Santa Barbara. Wrinkles started forming on the tips of my fingers.

"I feel like a prune," I said. "What time is it?" Bear looked at his waterproof wristwatch. "It's two-thirty," he said.

"I'd better get home."

"Okay. I've gotta be at work in an hour. By the way, what's the rush?" he asked.

"I promised Buffy I'd be there at three to help her with something."

On the trip home Santa Barbara was never mentioned again until I was about to jump out of the jeep. Then he said, "I won't bring it up again, I promise. You have four days to decide. I'll be leaving early Friday morning. If you decide to go with me, be waiting on the front steps at seven o'clock sharp. If I don't see you there, I'll know you decided to pass."

"It's more than going to Santa Barbara, you know." I wanted to explain. "I've never been with a boy like that before."

"Well, don't you trust me? Don't you know I care about you?"

"Yes, I do. I really do. But I have to feel right about it, no matter how much I care about you. So you see, it's not you. It's me. It's me and my mother."

"Your mother?" he said, surprised. "How did she get into it?"

"You know—guilt. Even though she's three thousand miles away I brought her with me. And I don't want to bring her to Santa Barbara because I think she'd have my hide."

"You're a big girl now. Isn't it time to leave your mother at home?"

"Maybe it is," I said. "I better go." I slammed the car door. The smell of gasoline flooded out of the exhaust as he turned the jeep around, then leaned out the window.

"I'll be driving this way on Friday morning. Maybe I'll see you then," he said, pulling away.

"Maybe," I answered under my breath. By that time the car was gone.

The house was quiet. The familiar scent of bitter orange from the oils the Byrons loved didn't keep away the anxiety that was building beyond control. It was too quiet. No music. No activity. Just sounds of an empty house. Buffy should be home any minute. I started eating sunflower seeds, then peanuts. I went upstairs, then downstairs to the front window. Somehow I thought if I envisioned Buffy walking up the front steps, she'd be home sooner. Magic or not, before long Buffy was jiggling her keys in the lock. Zack walked in with her. Buffy's face seemed light and somewhat pale.

"Are you all right?" I asked. She shook her head.

"Where's my mother?"

"She's not here, no one's home."

She sighed. "Good." I helped her upstairs. "I feel a little tired," Buffy admitted, "but I'm okay." I helped her into bed.

"Just rest," I said, taking her shoes off and helping her put her feet up.

She just sighed.

"I know how you feel," I said, and Buffy really was pleased I was there.

"Thank you for being home."

Zack poked his head in the room. "Be back in a little bit, have to do some things."

"I'll take care of her," I called. I closed the curtains to block out some of the sun shining in her eyes. "Can I do anything?" I asked.

"Oh, just sit here with me for a few minutes."

"Sure, as long as you like." Buffy noticed that I was just staring at her, my face filled with concern. "Hey, you're the one who's white as a sheet. Where's your smile, c'mon. Everything's gonna be all right. I'm fine now." At that moment we heard her mother come in the door, and soon Mom Byrons's voice was calling up the stairs.

"Girls, come on down a minute." Her voice was excited. Going to the head of the stairs, I yelled down, "Mom Byrons, Buffy's resting. She started jogging again today and she's exhausted. She always tends to overdo it. I bet she did five miles."

"Tell her plenty of rest is the best thing. Tell her to take the day off," she yelled back. The next thing we knew she was coming up the stairs, into Buffy's room, singing "Happy Birthday." She carried a beautiful pink birthday cake in the shape of a woven basket filled with a floral arrangement in butter cream and ablaze with candles. I had totally forgotten it was my birthday.

"Blow them out," Buffy said, playing the part. I took a deep breath and blew them all out, all but one. Mom Byrons cheered me on. "Come on, blow that one out, too. That's the one to grow on."

I stared at that one lit candle. "I think I've grown on that one already," I told her. Then I blew the candle out. It dawned on me then that for a little while I had stopped thinking about myself.

NINE

THE NEXT DAY BUFFY WAS TAKING IT SLOW AND I WAS KEEPING HER company. We pulled old yearbooks out of the closet and school projects from elementary school that Buffy had saved for posterity. In the junk was a tarnished picture frame with a photo of us dressed as fruitcakes for a street fair.

"Those berries were wilting right on my head," Buffy started to laugh.

"And look, there I am next to you with grapes dangling down—or were they raisins? Has Zack seen these?" I asked, holding the picture up to the window for better light.

"Let me see." She took a closer look and burst into hysterics. "Raisins! They're raisins! I can't show Zack everything. What do you think we play? Show and tell? Especially when I'm dressed as a fruitcake."

"I think at the next fair we should be vegetables," I said.

"Yes, I'd definitely be a zucchini."

All this silly talk wasn't helping me forget that I had three days to make up my mind what to do, and no fruit or vegetables were going to help. This was a good time to tell Buffy about Santa Barbara and my confusion. She mostly listened, then took out a piece of paper and in one column wrote down the positive part of going and in the other column the negative. We tried to take everything into consideration. My loving Bear and wanting to be with him was definitely leading on the positive side.

Top entry on the negative side was my emotional equipment. I wanted it to be right, right for me, that is. The main problem was that physically I knew that I was ripe for the picking but psychologically the soil still needed a little more cultivation. Which brought me directly to what was next on the negative side: I was scared to death of taking the plunge.

"There's always got to be a first time for everything," Buffy told me. "Even this."

"You make it sound like a swimming lesson," I said, nervously twisting my shirt around my index finger. "I must be regressing," I said, taking my hand away quickly.

Buffy nodded. "I have to agree," she said. "Look—I plunged and I surfaced." Seeing that I was still totally confused, she placed the list of pros and cons in the palm of her hand and pretended to weigh it. "I'd say both sides are equal," she concluded.

"So I'm back to square one." I took the paper from her and examined it more closely. "If I could only find the answer."

"You're a borderline case. You can go either way!" Buffy tipped her hand back and forth. "You have to listen to your instincts."

"Great!" I answered her. "My instincts have suddenly gone mute."

She laughed. "Temporary laryngitis, that's all."

The rest of the day we listened to records. Buffy rummaged through and cleaned out a few more junk drawers, while I wrote postcards home to some friends. Then the phone rang.

"Hello, Gab. Is that you?"

"Yes, Bear. It's me." I was happily surprised. I hadn't thought I would hear from him until Friday morning.

"My parents are having a dinner party tomorrow night, and this morning my mother realized she forgot to tell me about it. And she said, why don't I invite you to come. So . . . I was wondering . . ."

I interrupted, "Thanks, I'd love to."

"Good," he said. "I'll pick you up tomorrow at seven o'clock and I won't mention Friday, promise."

"See you then," I said, and we hung up. Buffy was sharpening some pencils. "You'd love to what?" she asked over the grinding sounds of the electric pencil sharpener.

"That was Bear," I said, smiling.

"I know, I know, what did he say?" she asked.

"He invited me to a dinner party at his house tomorrow night. His mother asked him to invite me."

"Well, la-de-da," Buffy said. "Making it into the family, are you?" There was a tinge of envy in her voice; maybe she thought I was moving up in the world.

"Oh, Buffy, I want them to like me so much."

"They won't like you," Buffy answered. "They'll love you."

"And he promised not to bring up Friday," I said with a sigh of relief.

114

"He's a gentleman, all right." Yes, I thought, maybe she was right.

Buffy insisted on spending the rest of the afternoon planning my outfit for the dinner party. We must have pulled out all of Buffy's clothes, trying on various combinations. Her bed was a rainbow of colors, and she seemed to be enjoying it more than me. Her sense of optimism had returned. After all the costume changes, we selected a wine-colored velvet caftan.

"It's you," Buffy said, placing a long strand of black and brown Moroccan beads over my head.

"It *is* me." I laughed, staring at myself in a mirror. After all that work Buffy had a craving for a rare roast beef sandwich with a side order of cole slaw from the delicatessen in town. I said I'd go get it for her, but she tried to talk me out of it. "No. You've got to have it," I said, putting my jeans back on. She handed me the keys to her car. "No, I'll walk to the corner and take the bus," I said. "I'll be back in no time."

I ran to the corner and caught the bus just in time. I took a seat near the window so I could watch for my stop. As the bus approached Westwood Boulevard, I saw the old lady with her shopping cart sitting on her bench. I quickly pulled the buzzer and ran to the rear exit.

As the bus pulled away, I sat down on the blue bench right next to her. She was bundled up in a few sweaters even though it must have been about eighty degrees out. I sat there a few minutes, then suddenly I found myself asking her, "Do you know if the Number 7 bus comes here?"

Close up she appeared near sixty years old, and her face was rough and crinkly. "You talking to me?" she asked in a loud voice. I was almost sorry I had said anything. "Yes," I answered softly.

"It doesn't stop in front of my bank," she said. I looked up at Great Western Savings Bank.

"Oh, do you keep your money here?" I asked.

"No, I live here."

She put her hand on the shopping cart, rocking it like a baby. "I wouldn't take any of your things," I said, watching how possessive she became. The shopping cart moved back and forth almost hypnotically. "You never know when you're going to need something. And it'll be right here," she said, pointing to her junk collection. "I can't be too careful, you know. Last month some creep came up from behind, to try to steal my life savings. I knocked him cold, like that." She socked her fist against her palm. "Slam."

Most of the bags were ripped and taped, some even tied up with cord; a pot handle poked out of one bag through a rip. She noticed me staring. "What are you staring at, Missy?" she asked, her voice tough. "That's my stuff you're staring at. Haven't you been told it's not nice to stare?"

"Oh, I'm sorry." I didn't want to offend her. "All your things are fascinating. Where did you collect them all?" She stopped rocking her cart, trying to determine if I was putting her on. Then her face grew proud as she looked over her possessions. "You'd be surprised what people throw out. I live on what people throw out. Perfect sweaters," she said, showing the wornout one she was wearing. "I collect sweaters. Wool. Angora. Everything."

I glanced over. "Very nice," I said.

"And I'm portable." She lifted her hands up. "Not tied down to any house or anything. There's other things, too. Some things still have price tags on them. Books. Magazines. I spend a lot of time reading," she said, pulling out a copy of Jane Austen's

Pride and Prejudice. "See, I found this one on the corner of Westwood and Sunset. Belonged to one of those college kids. I find lots of notes, too. Read 'em all. Messy handwriting, though. Wish they'd write neater."

"Wow," I said in amazement. "You never know what you're going to find."

"That's where the fun is, dearie. It's like archaeology. If I ever went back to school, I'd study that. Archaeology, I love collecting treasures, like this. I never throw anything out. I never know when I'm going to need it. Like that pot. One day, I said, I'm going to fill it up with water, and it's a good thing I did, because I got sick for a few days in January, a high fever, and I couldn't push my cart around, so I was glad to have my pot of water."

I listened to her, nodded in agreement, but I wished I could have been there to help her. I took out a piece of paper, scribbled fast. "Here. Here's my number. Call me if you get sick. I don't live too far away. Maybe I could bring you medicine or something."

Slowly she reached for the paper and started to read the numbers, then peered at me over the tattered paper.

"This you?" she asked. I nodded. She sat there almost frozen, like she was memorizing the number or she was insulted. Then she raised her head to me. "That's very nice of you," she said, stuffing the number in her sweater pocket. "I'll keep you in my pocket."

"I've got to go now," I said, standing up. I reached into my pocket and pulled out a five-dollar bill. "Can I give you this? Maybe you can have a good meal." I offered it to her.

She pushed my hand away. "No," she said. "I live on junk, not handouts." Her eyes became alive. "Sometimes people throw away money, the real McCoy. Especially pennies. They add up, you know. That's when I stock up on groceries." I was walking away when she called after me, "but if you're ever around here, I'll be glad to keep you company when you have lunch. You can buy me a cup of coffee. Hot coffee."

"You're on." I smiled and crossed the street.

When I came back Buffy told me my mother had called, and then tore open the bag with the roast beef on rye with a knish as a bonus. I bought two of everything to keep her company. The smell of knishes being reheated reminded me of home, and I found myself wanting to talk with my parents. I had just taken a bite when the phone rang and I answered.

"Hello, hello, Mom, it's me. How are you?"

"We wanted to wish you a late happy birthday. Did you spend it with Bear?"

For a split second I had this tremendous urge to blurt it all out, to tell her that we loved each other, that my feelings were snowballing inside, that a part of me wanted to go away with him overnight, but a part of me and a part of her were holding me back.

But I didn't. "I'm going to Bear's home for a dinner party. They invited me," I said.

"Oh. Are these going to be my future in-laws?" she asked jokingly.

I put the sandwich down. I had suddenly lost my appetite. "There you go, playing Cupid again."

"Here's Dad," she said. "He's pulling the phone away from me. I think he misses you like crazy."

"Happy birthday, baby," he sang out.

"Thank you, Daddy."

"Mother said something about a dinner party?"

118

"I'll tell you all about it next week," I said, "after I go."

"And what's this about you're in love, is that so?" he asked me, his tone playful.

"Well . . . I . . . I . . ." I stammered over my words.

"Just checking on my baby. By the way, honey, there's nothing wrong with being in love."

"Thanks, Dad." I changed the subject quickly.

When I hung up, Buffy turned to me. "Why are you so afraid to tell them you love Bear? It's not a crime."

"Maybe I'm afraid they'll spoil it."

Before I knew it the next day had passed and I was standing in front of the mirror pulling the wine caftan over my head. The necklace my mother had given me before I left home was buried under some shirts in my top drawer. The shiny gold necklace felt heavy to my touch and as I slipped it over my neck I vividly saw the pride on my mother's face as she offered this necklace to me. Now I realized what was in her eyes. I think she saw that I wasn't a child anymore.

Buffy studied the new addition. "It doesn't go."

"I like it," I said, straightening the chain out. "I'll wear it."

"I wonder who'll be there. Maybe some stars," Buffy said, as she watched me put on my mascara.

"What are you trying to do? Scare me half to death?" I said, laughing. "What could I possibly say to a star?"

"It's a Hollywood party, isn't it?"

"No! It's just a simple dinner party," I said. "That's what Bear said. Whatever that is. I've never been to one before."

"Well, stars need an audience. Act interested. Make believe you're listening. They'll walk away saying what a great conversationalist you were when you didn't even say a word."

"What do I talk about if they're *famous?*"

119

"Famous people are human, too."

"Are you sure about that?" I asked, and we laughed as Buffy sprayed me with Givenchy perfume.

"We've come a long way from Evening in Paris toilet water," I commented. "This is the big time."

The doorbell rang, and Buffy ran to the window. "Bear's got the Rolls-Royce!" she screamed.

"Oh, no!" I froze in my tracks.

"Come on," Buffy said, pushing me out the door. "Half of Long Island would change places with you in a second."

Bear took a few steps back. "Wow. You look great," he said.

"So do *you*."

The collar of his white shirt was open, spread over the lapels of his blue blazer. His hair was perfectly combed, his eyes very blue. I suddenly felt even more insecure. I found myself searching for some clue, a gesture, anything.

"My parents like you. They think you're sharp."

"I like them. A whole lot."

"And a lot of their friends are waiting to meet you."

"Me? Oh, no."

"Come on, don't worry. They're going to love you," he assured me, helping me into his parents' Rolls.

I saw Buffy watching from an upstairs window, and I blew her a kiss just as Zack pulled up to the curb and did a double-take. "Yes, it's us," I said, as we pulled out.

When we arrived at Bear's house it was ablaze with lights and tinseled grownups, elegantly dressed and loaded with jewelry. We had hardly walked in the door when a waiter, dressed in a black uniform and holding a tray of beautiful long-stemmed glasses, walked up to us.

"Champagne?"

Bear handed me a glass and took one for himself. He held his glass up to mine, "To *us*."

"To us," I repeated, and we clicked glasses. Bear linked his arm through mine as we sipped the champagne. I thought of the toast Buffy and I had made together on my sixteenth birthday, when Buffy wished for love and I wished to be free. And here I was now, clicking glasses thousands of miles from home with a boy my mother and father barely knew existed, yet who was the most important person in my life. One I was hoping to spend the rest of my life with. I took another sip and I beamed.

"What are you smiling about?"

"I'm happy. Very happy."

"Good. That's the whole idea."

A lady in a white uniform interrupted, serving hors d'oeuvres. "Would you like a rumaki?" I sought a translation from Bear.

"Chicken livers wrapped in bacon," he said, popping one into his mouth. "Good! Try one."

Bear's father came over to say hello, but was called away almost immediately into a group of important-looking men. I watched a lady across the room. Partridge feathers grew out of her white angora sweater and framed her face! She was telling everyone she sewed the feathers on the sweater herself. When she sat down on the couch I whispered across to Bear, "I think she's getting ready to lay an egg."

Another woman was dressed in a gold lamé evening pants outfit right out of *Vogue* magazine. Another wore a diamond ring as big as a billiard ball. Most of the men looked like carbon copies of each other, in fitted dinner jackets and white pants, holding highball glasses. One of the conversations I overheard was a discussion of root rot. I wondered how the wives could tell them all apart.

"Having a nice time?" Bear quizzed me.

"Yes," I said, biting into a piece of raw carrot, the only thing in the room that made me feel at home.

When his mother saw us, she came over and gave me a very theatrical hug.

"Have you met *everyone?*"

Bear put his arm around me. "We're making our way around the room," he said. What really impressed me was that she could be having a good time at her own party. My mother would have been running in and out of the kitchen the entire night.

The woman in the starched white uniform came around again. "What's that?" I asked, looking at crispy things on a silver tray.

"Breaded frog legs."

"No thank you," I said, managing to smile.

"Dinner is served," Bear's mother announced as she came around to usher her guests in to dinner. The table was beautiful! Eight candles of different heights were surrounded by flowers. I was about to sit down when Bear said, "Let's see where your name card is." We walked around the table. To my surprise Bear and I weren't sitting together. And his mother and father were too far away to get involved in an intimate conversation.

"Here," he said, holding the chair out for me.

"Where are you going to sit?" I asked in fright.

"Within walking distance," he said, walking around the table.

"I'd rather it were within talking distance," I answered.

Nobody was sitting with their mates or dates or ex-husbands. My dinner partner on the left was a balding man, slightly on the feminine side, who owned a men's boutique on Rodeo Drive. Our conversation lasted two minutes at most as we strained to find something in common.

Then I found myself talking to the man on my other side, a

Mr. Clay Olsen. "I'd like you to meet Mrs. Olsen, the Fourth," he said, trying to get his wife's attention across the table and down two seats. It turned out to be the bird lady.

"You mean you're the fourth generation of Clay Olsens?" I asked.

"No, no, no, my dear," he said, patting my hand as if I were a child. "She's my fourth wife."

One lady spoke only of the difficulty of finding good help; the only thing her maid could relate to was the floors. The man across the table was discussing his latest big business deal. He'd bought a new oil well a few yards away from the Beverly Hills High School football field that week, and then came home to find his wife, now his separated wife, having a match with the tennis pro, only the match wasn't on the tennis court. He winked at his date, an eighteen-year-old starlet-type, with gold glitter on her eyelids. A lady at the other end of the table debated whether to slip off to Bali with her masseur for her divorce celebration or throw a catered party at home.

The only couple that really seemed together were Bear's parents. I tried to make a good impression on them, even though we were sitting at opposite ends of the table and I used the wrong fork for the appetizer and spilled my glass of wine. Thank goodness there wasn't much left. And through all the feathers, and Bali, and terra-cotta floors, oil wells, and the fourth Mrs. Olsen, I kept wondering whether to go away with Bear in a few days. Maybe it was a small decision compared to what others around this table seemed to be going through. But for me it was my whole life. I didn't want to make a mistake like all the Mrs. Olsens. I wanted to stay the First. I was wondering, too, what I was doing at this table.

Just then Bear smiled across the table. He could see I was

uncomfortable. He made a face and shrugged his shoulders, as if to say, "Me, too." We hurried through the veal medallions and puffed potatoes and apple sabayon. By the time the waitress came around with strawberries and orange peels dipped in chocolate, Bear came over and pulled out my chair.

"We've got to be going," he said. Containing my jubilance, I followed him. "Goodnight, everyone," he said, and we ran out the door.

As soon as we were out of earshot we broke into hysterical laughter. "Have you ever been so bored in your life?" Bear asked between gasps, handing me some chocolate-covered strawberries he had stuffed in his pocket.

"I thought it was just me," I said, taking a chocolate. "All these people trading in their lives so quickly. Why?" I asked him.

"I guess some people are in a rush," he said.

"A rush. For what?"

"A rush to try the next thing. I mean, if it's not working, it's not working." He took my hand and we started down the path.

"Don't you have to *make* it work sometimes?" I protested.

He stopped me short, and kissed me. "Sure you do," he said.

What a relief it was to be out in the fresh air, with something as real as the stars twinkling and a moon just on the wane.

"Come on, get in," he said, climbing up in his jeep.

"Where are we going?" I asked, holding up my long caftan so I could take the large step up.

"To the Renaissance Fair," he shouted. Then I remembered Buffy and looked at my watch.

"You going to turn into a pumpkin?"

"I was just wondering what Buffy and Zack were up to."

124

"Well, why don't we go find out? Maybe they'll come," he suggested.

"Great idea," I answered.

We drove to the house and rang the bell before opening the door. "Bear and I are here," I yelled as we went in.

"We're in here," Zack yelled back from the den. Buffy was playing "Chopsticks" on the piano. "Dinner party over so early?" She stopped playing.

"It was a bore," Bear said.

"Lots of birds and feathers and Olsens to the fourth power," I started telling her.

"Want to go to the Renaissance Fair for a nightcap?" Bear interrupted.

"Sure," they answered. Buffy ran upstairs to change her clothes and came down tying a green brocade ribbon in her hair. "I'm ready for the Renaissance," she said.

TEN

THE NIGHT WAS WARM AND BALMY AS WE DROVE ALONG SILENTLY, enjoying the darkness and the quiet. Bear was the first to talk. "I'm glad we're getting to the fair. It's the last night."

We drove for another half hour or so and then there it was, the Renaissance Fair, standing out like a circus in the middle of the dark, barren hills.

The sounds of bagpipes and trumpeters heralded our arrival. Banners with bright English seals unfurled in the evening breeze and the smell of sausage and pastry drifted through the parking lot. A girl dressed in a long brocaded dress and high-frilled collar walked arm and arm with a boy in a crimson velvet robe.

Rustic booths covered with burlap cloth were scattered for

miles up and down the rolling hills. I was glad to leave the twentieth century and the thought of Friday behind me for a while, and walk into the Renaissance.

A jester in tights and tunic at the entrance sang out, "Get ye here. Begone dull cares. 'Tis time for the faire. Yes, you little lovely wench ripe for picking," he said, picking me out of the group. "Slummin', are ya?" he said to me and Bear. I laughed, putting my arm through his as we walked into the bustling marketplace.

"Bright shiny ribbons for the lady's hair. Fine trinkets to wear," a young woman said, holding out a colorful wreath made of dried flowers, with long colorful ribbons streaming down.

"Sherri?" he said, like he had met her before.

"Hi there," she giggled.

"Working here?" he asked her.

"I need the bread, between commercials."

"We'll take *two*," Bear said, paying the girl. Buffy and I selected purple and pink dried flowers with baby's breath.

"Who is she?" I asked him as we walked away.

"Oh, I just met her at a flower shop," he said lightly, then took my wreath and placed it on my head.

"Brains for sale! Brains for sale!" I heard someone call. Then a peddler caught our attention. "What's your pleasure?" he asked. His cheeks were rosy like a Brueghel painting, and pots and pans clanked around his body.

"A lovely night for a midsummer's eve wedding! Marry for the day," he went on. Then, taking and placing my hand over Bear's, said, "And now I take these two lovers, on their way to be wed. In the eyes of friends and neighbors, high-born and low, and in this bond of reverie, I pronounce thee man and wife." He reached into one of his pots and sprinkled flower petals over us like magic dust. He gave us each a slug of ale. And for a split second, I believed him and walked away under the spell of our mock marriage.

"Always the best man, never the groom," Zack said, teasing us.

"He probably picked us because you two look like you're old married people already," I said.

"Aren't you going to kiss the bride?" Buffy teased.

"Let's Drench a Wench," Zack suggested, pointing to a buxom lady suspended over a large barrel. "Come all, the young, the old, the undecided," a guy beckoned us on.

"No, let's eat. I'm starved." Bear started toward the food stalls.

"Me, too," I said.

"Gabrielle and I'll get on line for the food. You guys get the ales," Buffy said.

"I want that giant turkey leg, the biggest they've got," Bear ordered.

"Get me some roast beef," Zack called out.

Buffy and I carried the food to some bales of hay and we ate like greedy peasants while a young girl plucked at her harp and sang songs of lost love.

It was Bear's and my second dinner of the evening, but this dinner was very different. No chocolate-covered orange peels or delicate linen napkins here.

By this time the crowd was really loosening up. People were drinking and singing and dancing in between the stalls, on the bales of hay. Voices were growing louder, building into a frenzy, the actors leading the way.

A gypsy woman across the way caught my eye. She beckoned me with her finger. I had always wanted to have my fortune told, and hoped she'd provide some answers for me. "I'll be right back," I said.

Bear laughed as he watched me go to the gypsy. She held up her Tarot cards like a shield. "Come inside," she said with an accent, pulling aside a purple curtain. A sign said five dollars, so I handed the money to her and she placed it quickly in the pocket of her dress. She laid the Tarot cards out face down, her fingers limber in their movements, as though attuned to what lay beneath. Then she shuffled the cards and asked me to cut the deck.

"Pick the first ten cards and turn them face down," she instructed.

She turned the first card over. It looked like a queen sitting on a throne. "It's the card of *kindness*," she said. The next card was a prince petting a lion. "This indicates great firmness and intensity in you," she said. "I see you're not from California. Not from this area. You're from the East. New York."

Big deal, I thought, my accent was a real giveaway.

Then she turned over the Ace of Coins. "I see an engagement," she spoke in a trance. "Marriage is in store for you. I see, too, that you've met someone recently you care very much about."

"Yes, I have," I answered.

"See that Ace?" she said. "That signifies the beginning of love. And I see money. Lots of money. You're going to be very, very comfortable." She flipped over another card. "And I see three children in the stars for you." She smiled. "You're going to be very busy, too."

I loved what she was saying and could have listened forever.

The small light accentuated her angular face as she concentrated, turning over the next card. "I see Hope. Things in your life which have been causing disharmony are going to iron out; there seems to be something bothering you but it will resolve itself. Your future seems very promising. I see it here in the cards," she said, tapping one.

Just then a couple pulled the purple curtain aside. "Hey, are you going to be in there all day?" they asked.

"Just one minute," the gypsy yelled. Then she turned back to me. "That's it," she said abruptly, gathering up the Tarot cards.

Bear was waiting patiently. "What'd she say?"

"Oh, nothing much," I answered. "Just about love and babies and that sort of thing. Where're Zack and Buffy?"

"They were following some soothsayer down the road. They said they'd be back here in five minutes, to wait for them. Are you sure she said nothing all that time?"

"Just silly stuff."

The fair was winding up in a frenzy of noise. Suddenly the flutes, the trumpets, and the singing balladeers all blurred together in a loud shrill sound as the festivities reached their peak on the last night. And, rather than this frenetically charged final hour, Bear and I desperately wanted to be by ourselves.

We found a darkened corner behind a stall and gave into the heightened sense of pleasure we found with each other. He pulled me into his arms and kissed me and I kissed him back till we were caught up in our own frenzy. Then we stopped suddenly, and he whispered in my ear, "I love you."

"And I love you," I finally told him. I couldn't believe how easily the words flowed out.

Sensing violence just beneath the surface gaiety, Buffy and Zack returned to the designated meeting spot, forcing us out of our hiding place at an inopportune moment.

We all agreed that the fair was in its final seconds and it was time to leave the seventeenth century. Bear and I walked with our arms tightly around each other. By the time we reached the exit, many of the stalls were closing down for the next show in another state, another place.

When we got to the car, Bear and Zack were making plans.

"Let's go to the watering hole," Bear suggested.

"No, Bear, let's head back. I'm tired," I said, slipping my shoes off.

"All right. All right. The old girl's tired," he said.

"A few hours ago I was just a young maiden," I said, smiling.

Bear seemed too drunk to drive, but so did Zack and Buffy.

"Why don't you let me drive?" I suggested, although I was scared of driving in the dark through high cliffs and winding canyon roads.

"You're not allowed to drive, remember?" Bear said.

"But *I'm* the one who's sober."

Bear took the wheel. "Welcome back to the twentieth century," he said, taking a hairpin turn much too quickly. He skidded around another one and I felt sure we'd all fall off the cliff. My eyes were glued to the road every fraction of the way, and I held on to the dashboard for dear life. I wasn't ready to die, not yet.

Finally, we turned off the dark canyon road onto Pacific Coast Highway. The sight of headlights from oncoming traffic made me nearly sob with relief. "We made it," I sighed as Buffy's house came into sight. For a moment there I had felt that this was the end.

"Did you really think we wouldn't make it?" Bear asked, and everyone laughed, everyone but me.

The coyotes were howling some distance away, that piercing cry, the cry of the kill. "There must be a full moon," Zack said, as we hopped out of the jeep. He held the door open for Buffy and me, which only accentuated the fact that Bear was continuing on alone.

"Goodnight everyone." He pouted slightly. "You sure know how to make a guy feel real lonely." Then he drove down the street into the dark night.

ELEVEN

THURSDAY NIGHT I KEPT TOSSING BACK AND FORTH, TRYING to figure out what I'd do in the morning. Bear would be by early.

There was a noise downstairs, a cupboard door closing. I jumped up and listened. My lifeline. Whoever it was, I hoped they were friendly at two in the morning.

Tiptoeing down the stairs, I followed the whistling of a tea kettle into the kitchen. Mom Byrons jumped. "So there's someone else who couldn't sleep," she said, smiling. "An insomniac loves company." She put some loose tea into a spoon with holes and dipped it in a cup. "Would you like a nice warm cup of camomile tea?"

I wondered why *she* couldn't sleep when she seemed such a

calm person. Maybe she knew about Buffy or maybe she felt something was wrong.

"Do you have tea every morning at two?" I asked, playing detective.

"There's a full moon tonight. It always wakes me up." She peered out the kitchen window.

Thoughts were whirling around in my mind. "Mom Byrons, can I ask you something?"

"You can ask me anything. You're my second daughter."

"I have a problem."

Her eyes opened wide, and a faint smile came to her lips. She loved solving problems. Lifting her cup to her mouth, she took a sip. "Welcome to the club. Is it Bear?"

"He has to go to Santa Barbara overnight to scout some movie locations, and he wants me to go *with* him."

"What's the problem?" she asked me.

"Well, I don't know if I should go. I've never been away with a boy overnight. You know what I mean."

She smiled. "I know, sweetheart. Do you love him?"

I nodded. "Yes, I do. And I'm attracted to him, but I haven't made up my mind about sex yet. I've been putting off thinking about it, and here it is."

"I know you want me to provide an answer for you," she said, "but I can't do that, Gabrielle."

"But I'm so confused." I nearly moaned. "I don't know what to do."

"The answer lies in *you*. Just listen to your own voice," she said, taking another sip of her tea. "When you go back to bed, lie there and listen. You've made up your mind already; all that's left is hearing what it is."

"I have?" I asked.

"Yes. Just allow yourself to hear it."

"But how do I do that?"

"You start by quieting yourself down."

I waited for her to go on. She lifted her hand up in the air and moved it slowly before she talked. "There's a little language in us which has no name, no words, just feelings in our body. Part of our job is deciphering them, understanding what they are. All those tingles and sensations mean something. Those flushes of blood running to your head, butterflies in your stomach, jumpy feelings. That's your voice without words. It's up to you to give it words. Whatever words you want. But it's a language that doesn't lie."

"How do I learn it?" I asked, leaning forward.

She smiled. "You learn to speak it by listening to yourself. By beginning to give words to those feelings in your body. And soon you begin to recognize it: oh, that's fear. Or that's pain. Sometimes your body even tells you it's angry. You can't deny that feeling, because that's important, too," she said, pouring some more tea in my blue mug and then in hers.

"I don't know any of that stuff."

"You will. It's part of growing up."

"If grown-ups know that language how come they've never told me about it?"

"Who said all grown-ups know it?" she asked. I sat there and shook my head.

"If you decide to go, move into it," she said.

"Move into it?" I questioned her.

She looked at my quizzical face. "In other words, enjoy yourself," she said, planting a kiss on the top of my head.

My eyelids were getting heavy, almost closing over my half-drunk tea. Some of the tea leaves had sunk to the bottom and

I swirled them around with my spoon, watching them sink again. I got up, rinsed my cup out, and gave Mom Byrons a hug. "I think I'll try to sleep now."

"At least you have a choice. If you decide to go, call me from Santa Barbara. If not, I'll see you at breakfast," she said.

I walked away deep in thought. It was three-thirty in the morning. In New York, it would be six-thirty in the morning. My father would be perking the coffee and finishing some paperwork.

And here I was lying in Buffy's house, trying to end my day while they were beginning the next. In a funny way, I wished I were back home in my own bed; my mother would come to me when I just awakened, and we'd talk in our early-morning voices of silly things that we may never have mentioned once the day actually began. We called it "dreamtalking," even though it was about things we were dreaming of after we had awakened.

I curled up into a ball and pulled the blanket over my head. I felt chilly, yet the room was warm. Mom Byrons's words kept haunting me, and I tried to hear my own self speak. Other voices kept interrupting each other with four a.m. conversations in my head, clashing, yelling at each other, trying to win a point. My mother. My father. Buffy. Bear. And lastly Mom Byrons's reassuring suggestion that I knew the answer already—all I had to do was listen.

It was now four-thirty and I kept watching the digital clock, watching the minutes and seconds of the night go by. At seven o'clock my alarm went off. Dawn was breaking through the palm trees. Somehow I had survived the night. All my confusion was gone, and I knew what I wanted to do.

Bear said he'd be by at seven-thirty. That left only a half-hour. The house was silent. I heard a newspaper hit the front door. I thought Buffy might have gotten up early for a glass of juice or something, so I tiptoed across the hall. Mr. Byrons was a very light sleeper.

Buffy's door was closed and I listened to Zack's breathing for a few seconds.

It was so quiet I heard the click from the digital clock changing to seven-fifteen. Quickly I got dressed. I knew Bear would be coming any moment. Every step seemed to creak as I ran downstairs. I sat on the front steps, the intense morning sun blinding my eyes, which were riveted to the corner, waiting for Bear's jeep to make the turn. I waited. No cars. A few leaves had fallen from the magnolia bush, and I folded them like origami paper until they split apart and some of the juice came oozing out on my fingers. It made my fingers sticky. No jeep yet. Did he think I wasn't going and pass the street altogether? I opened the paper. The president was having a press conference tonight. They were expecting a heat wave through most of the United States, and in New York the day would be a scorcher.

The brilliant orange birds of paradise, delphiniums, and gardenias opening up seemed to be the only things awake. I poked my head inside. It wasn't even seven thirty-five. And suddenly, there he was.

"Hey, can I give you a lift?" Bear yelled to me in a loud whisper. He looked particularly handsome this morning, and I wanted to be with him more than ever.

"Are you getting in?" he asked, opening the door for me.

Instead, I walked around to his side of the jeep. "I'm not going."

"Is this a joke?" he asked.

My hands were in my pockets, pulling them down so hard I thought the pockets would rip apart. "No joke," I said, shaking my head.

"Okay," he said, closing the door he had opened for me. His voice was angry, his exuberance gone.

"But don't you want to know why I'm not going?" I asked, not wanting him to be angry with me.

He turned cold, as cold as I had felt last night under the blankets. "I'm listening," was his response.

"I want to be with you but I haven't made up my mind about . . . about . . ."

He cut me off. "You told me you love me."

"I do." But it was like he didn't hear me.

His eyes betrayed a sense of rejection. Or hurt. Perhaps it was more that I was reading my feelings into him.

"Well, I've never been away with a boy before and I'm afraid. And I don't know if I can handle it. I mean I know I can go to bed with you—that's easy to do—but can I deal with it afterward? That's the part I don't know. Do you understand what I'm saying?" I looked into his eyes. Anyway, that's what I felt. And I wanted to trust it.

"Isn't it time for you to grow up?" he asked coolly.

"I don't think that's the problem."

"You're old-fashioned!" he yelled at me. "Everyone does it."

"Everyone might, but I'm not everyone!" I yelled back.

"Well," he said, pausing a moment, "Gabrielle, I have a reservation at the Miramar Hotel tonight, and I'm going to keep it." He pointed to himself. "This person will be spending the afternoon in the sun with you or without you."

I backed away from the jeep and watched him throw it into first gear.

"I'll see you when you grow up." Then he sped away.

He was nearly around the corner. "Good-bye," I said, watching him drive out of my life.

TWELVE

THE HOUSE WAS STILL. EVERYONE WAS FAST ASLEEP. IT WASN'T even eight o'clock yet, and already the day was ruined. Was I afraid of my own shadow? Was I afraid of moving on? What did I do? I'd ruined it all. I kept torturing myself with my own words. I never cared so much about a person and I ruined it. I wanted to cry, and yet I felt angry at the same time. I picked up a purple pillow and started squeezing it with all my might until all the cotton filling squished together.

"That pillow's taken quite a beating. I hit that one often," Buffy said, walking toward me.

"I ruined it," I kept repeating.

"You didn't ruin anything. What did you ruin?" she asked.

"Oh, you should have seen him." The pillow wouldn't return to its original shape no matter how I pushed it.

"Come on. Put the pillow down," she said, taking me into the kitchen for a glass of juice. She opened the refrigerator and poured some for both of us. "What did he say?"

" 'Grow up!' That's what he said. 'Grow up.' Do you think I'm just retarded or something?"

"Mmmm," she said, taking a sip of her juice, then licking her lips. "Do you?" She answered my question with a question.

"No, of course not!" My emotions broke through. "I don't think that not being ready for something is being retarded."

"You know, he might have really been looking forward to going away and everything. I'm sure that he'll cool down during the two-hour drive and call you when he finishes his work up there. He'll call. You'll see."

"Oh, no. I don't think he will."

"Can I ask you something, Gabby? Why didn't you go? I kind of thought you might."

"You did?"

"Yeah."

"I know him less than a month. How do I know it's going to last?"

She opened the kitchen window, a soft breeze blew in. "There are no guarantees."

"So, you think I should have gone, huh?"

"I know what I would have done. . . . You don't have to do anything you don't want to do, right? I mean, you can be alone with him in bed and just hold hands if that's all you want to do, right. Right?" She said waiting for an answer.

"That couldn't happen. I'm too attracted to him. Oh, this is the real thing. And I'm making such a mess."

"You're not making a mess."

"I wish I had your courage."

"Courage," she laughed. "Courage has nothing to do with it. You've got what it takes—*instinct*. It's a gut reaction."

"You make it sound so natural."

"Well, it is!"

"All I hear is *don't*s. Don't do this. Don't do that. I don't know if it's me saying it or my mother. I'm so confused."

"Listen." Buffy nudged me with her elbow. "Your mother didn't raise you to be a nun. And don't you remember, you couldn't wait to get away. Remember that toast you made on your birthday? To be free. Well, be free."

I walked to the window and stared out. "Well, it's not as easy as I thought."

"There's always a first time. Bear invited *you*, not your mother. Do you want to be with him?"

"Yes. Yes, I do."

"Let Mother Nature do her work. And don't worry."

"Oh, Buffy. It was easier when we could laugh about it. But now that it's so close . . . You know, Buffy, I care about Bear more than I ever thought was possible and it's stronger than anything I've ever known before."

"I told you that you weren't immune to the disease when you first arrived here."

"Well, you were right, but now look at me. I'm dying of it!"

Buffy turned to me. "I know a good cure—you can change your mind." Buffy's eyes had a devilish look, baiting me.

"Buffy, I don't think so."

"Why not?"

"I don't think I should go."

"Go ahead, surprise him."

"Do **you** think I really should?"

"You're so depressed, it'll lift your spirits."

I sank into the living room couch and put my hands over my face and muttered to myself.

"I have a great idea," Buffy said, her eyes lighting up. "Why don't I help you pack a picnic lunch. It's still early enough in the day; you can bring it up to him in two hours. Take the lead. You don't have to sit around waiting for him to call you. Times have changed. You're his girlfriend."

"Past tense. Was his girlfriend."

"C'mon, take a chance, show him how you feel."

"He knows how I feel; I don't think that's the problem."

"So what's the problem?" Buffy asked me.

"I don't even think I know what the problem is anymore. I'm so confused and depressed. I've ruined it all, haven't I?"

Buffy sat there, staring at me. "So why don't you go?"

"Where's the picnic basket?"

"Then you'll go?" Buffy said excitedly.

I jumped up off the couch. "C'mon," I said. "Let's hurry before I change my mind."

Buffy went to the pantry and pulled out the picnic basket. She threw out most of the contents. "You don't need this." Out came the forks and knives. In went a small checkered tablecloth and matching napkins.

"What's that for?"

"A French picnic. My parents take it to the Hollywood Bowl concerts."

"It looks good."

"Now you need a bottle of wine." Buffy pulled a long green bottle from her father's bar. "Soave Bolla 1979, a good year." She tucked the bottle in the basket.

"I've never tried Soave Bolla," I said.

"Neither have I," she said, laughing, "but I like the sound of it."

I watched her tuck the bottle snugly into the basket. "I think he's got a bottle already."

"Who cares? That's part of the magic, do the unexpected. Bring a bottle of wine to the person who least expects it. And some glasses, long-stemmed." She carefully wrapped the napkins around them. "Please bring these back, though—my mother's attached to them."

"I will, promise. Let's see now, what food? What about cheese?"

"There's an uncut piece of brie in the refrigerator. And, of course, bread." Buffy rummaged through the pantry and pulled out a box of unsalted nuts and threw it in, too. "Now some grapes—you can peel them for him!" Buffy buckled the basket closed. "There it is," she said, "all ready to go."

I picked up the basket and was about to head out the door when Buffy stopped me short.

"Put it down, you can't go like that. You've got to freshen up, it's part of the picture."

"Okay, but hurry," I said. "What if he's gone by the time I get there?"

"He won't be," she assured me. "Give him a few hours to spot locations, then he'll be in the sun." We dashed up to my room and pulled out about fifteen different changes of clothes. "Okay," I asked, "which should I wear?" holding up a blue dress with a little lace around the edge.

"No, no," she said, "not that drab dress, that's too straight." She rummaged through the clothes hanging in the closet. "Here, take this pink one, this is nice." I threw off my pants and slipped the dress over my head. My nerves had taken over now. I straightened the dress and put two barettes in my hair to hold the hair off my face. Buffy was still getting the picture straight. She went over to my dress and started clipping a pin into the middle of it. "Let's tuck it in here a little," she said, giving it a deeper cut, exposing more cleavage.

"That's deep enough," I said, slapping her hands. "I don't want to get raped, I just want to talk about my feelings."

She started running around me in a circle, spraying Eau de Joy like it was room freshener. "There, now you're ready," she said.

"Ready as I can get," I said, running down the stairs.

"Oh," Buffy remembered, "some incense."

"I don't need that," I said. "It's your mother's supply, anyway."

"No, it's not my mother's, it came from The Mother in the ashram," she explained.

"No, thanks, too many mothers spoil the broth," I said, rushing to the door, jingling the keys in my hand. And I read the inscription on the keys out loud. "*Mi casa es su casa*. My house is your house. You know, Buffy, maybe it is."

"Hurry," she said, pushing me out the door.

"Do I look all right?"

"You look, well, you look up front and terrific."

"Wish me luck," I said, running down the stairs and out the door.

"Take some flowers, dear," a voice said from the upstairs window. It was Mom Byrons. I did as she said, then snipped a gardenia off the bush and tucked it behind my ear.

Buffy ran after me down the steps, waving something in her

hand. "Here," she said, "take this, you'll need a map." The map was a little torn and weatherbeaten, and a coffee stain had totally wiped out Palm Springs, but I wasn't going to Palm Springs anyway. Buffy took a pen and marked my route. "You can't get lost," she instructed. Then she gave me an affectionate punch on my arm. "Here's mud in your eye, kid."

THIRTEEN

ONCE ON THE FREEWAY I KEPT ON ROUTE 405. THE MAP WAS THE ONLY thing I had to turn to when I wondered what I was actually doing driving head on into Santa Barbara. Did he still want to be with me, and would he actually be there at the hotel, I wondered? The trip went quickly. Before I knew it I saw signs signaling Santa Barbara ahead. Large, rugged rocks dotted the Pacific Coast; the waves beat against the gray stone jetty, then sprayed water high in the air.

Santa Barbara exit—two miles. I pulled off the freeway, up the road to the Miramar Hotel. My adrenaline had started pumping, *boom, boom, boom.* And there I was as I had imagined. Yet, there was no guarantee that Bear would actually be there.

A young girl in her early twenties looked up at me from the

reception desk. "Can I help you?" Her voice sounded friendly enough.

"I have something to deliver to Brad Randolph." I tried to keep my eyes from staring away nervously.

She turned around and hit some keys into the computer. "He's in Room 37." She smiled. "Go past the tennis courts— it's on the beach. If you get your feet wet you've gone too far."

"Thank you," I said, having gotten past the first step. It was all going as planned. Buffy was a genius.

I walked to the car and pulled out the basket and the flowers and wondered if Bear would still be angry with me.

"Nice flowers," a lady in a very large sun hat commented as I walked by. I smiled back, but the last thing I wanted was to be noticed. However, for all intents and purposes I could be a guest like anyone else. I imagined our conversation. Bear would be thrilled to see me, and he'd realize how quick he had been to lose his temper and judge me.

The tennis courts were to my right and rooms faced onto it, rooms that appeared older than I had expected, less glamorous. My basket was growing heavy. Somewhere in one of those rooms running along the beach in a row was Bear. I seriously considered running back to the car, but my momentary flight into panic was outweighed by anticipating our reunion.

To my surprise, there, across the yellow-green grass, was a locomotive and a set of railroad tracks. How odd, I thought, to have a locomotive museum right here on the grounds of a resort hotel. They must have thought it added charm. The ocean rooms were a few yards away. For a split second I stopped, switched the basket from one hand to the other, and took a deep breath. The fresh sea air was invigorating.

I crossed a set of railroad tracks and there on the other side was Bear's room. It did seem odd that they never removed the tracks when they built this hotel, though. It smelled damp along the walkway, almost like the ocean ran through the rooms. I walked along a row of rooms on the beach and stopped in front of his, the 7 slightly below the 3, the warped door slightly aged from the weather. I put the basket down. All that stood between us now were a few inches of wood—and my whole life. I flattened down a few creases in my dress, but it just didn't want to flatten out. Finally I mustered up enough courage to knock on the door. The tap was light at first. Two times. Silence. There was no answer and then I knocked again. That's when I heard footsteps.

"Yes." He was there. I wanted a loving reunion, and I prayed he wasn't going to be angry with me, that he would be as happy to see me as I would be to see him.

"Who is it?" he asked. But I didn't answer. I wanted to surprise him. I knocked again. I heard him undo the latch, and he peeked out. "Gabrielle," he exclaimed, "what are you doing here?" His hair was all messy. His eyes had a faraway look.

"Did I wake you?" I asked, somewhat flustered.

"No, no, not really," he said, coughing a little nervously. Yet he wasn't opening the door completely.

"Well, what is it?" I asked, "you don't want to see me?" His behavior seemed odd. And then in the back of the room, I saw a girl wrapped in a towel.

"Who is it?" she asked in a squeaky voice, almost a giggle.

"A friend of mine," he called back to her. "Gabrielle, you remember Sherri, the girl I introduced you to at the Renaissance Fair. She was selling wreaths."

"Oh, yes, I remember now," I said.

"Come in." He opened the door all the way. The girl stood

up and tucked her towel tighter. "Hey, c'mon in, we're having some pizza. There's plenty here, more than we can finish," she said with another giggle.

Bear took my arm and gave me a little push in the door. "C'mon in," he said.

"All right," I answered. I followed him into the room, playing with a piece of strap from the basket. Then Bear pulled out a chair and held it out for me.

"Have a seat," he said, as if we were at a dinner party.

Sherri ran toward the window and returned with plates and paper napkins. We're improvising," she explained. "I can't cook beans." She started to fold a napkin neatly. I handed it back to her.

"I brought my own," I said, taking a checked napkin out of the basket.

Bear pulled a piece of pizza from the pie and placed it on my plate.

"No, I have my own plate, too, thank you," I said, pulling it out of the basket. Sherri continued eating her pizza. I watched her pull a rubbery strand of cheese until it was two feet from her mouth.

"This is a long one." She laughed and gobbled it up all the way. I watched her. Who is she and why is she here? Did they have any relationship at all? It seemed at the Renaissance Fair that they hardly knew each other. How did she wind up here, I wondered, watching her across the table firmly wrapped in her white towel with the word "Miramar" going vertically down the front. With Bear in a skimpy bathing suit I felt overdressed for this party.

"It's very good pizza," I said, making conversation.

"Double cheese," she answered, placing a hand on Bear's

shoulder. "We worked up an appetite, didn't we?" She winked at Bear, her eyes glued to him.

"You're not eating any pizza," he said to me.

"I ate along the way," I lied.

I wanted to rush out of the room but something was keeping me there. I had to find out more about this girl and why she was here.

"Here's some more stuff," I announced, pulling out the wine glasses.

Little Bo Peep held the glass in her hand. "Quite a picnic basket you've got here."

"I don't need it anymore; my picnic's been cancelled," I said directly to Bear. His eyes squinted like they did when he got caught.

She picked up the bottle of wine. "Well, in that case . . ." She giggled again. As a matter of fact, I noticed she seemed to laugh at everything, even things that weren't funny.

"Thank you for the wine." Bear's tone held no sincerity at all.

Her long red nails curved around the bottle. "Ooh, Soave," she breathed. Bear took it and I handed him a corkscrew from the basket.

Sherri watched me take out the treats I had brought for Bear and me. The cheese, bread, the nuts. "You thought of every-thing," she said, "everything."

"Not everything," I answered. "I only brought two glasses." Bear got a glass from the bathroom and filled all three glasses with wine.

When we finished drinking it, I gathered up the two stemmed glasses. "Excuse me," I said, placing the glasses back into the wicker basket. "If you'll just excuse me," I said, standing up.

Just then the walls started to shake. The loud noise was deafening, and the room vibrated under me. We all looked at each other in astonishment; Bear opened the door in time to see a freight train whizzing by five feet from the room. All I could make out were patterns and colors. We watched until the train passed. Then Sherri turned to me. "Don't you want the wine? It's yours."

"All I want to do is get out of here." The cap was blowing off my emotions.

But she still tried to hand me the bottle, offering it as if it were a gift. I pushed it away. "Enjoy it, the two of you." And I bolted out of the door.

FOURTEEN

I HEADED FOR THE BEACH. THE PIERCING CRIES OF THE GULLS WERE soothing after that room. I was tired of the charade. Now I wanted to run, run as far as I could, away from it all. I felt like screaming. Instead I kicked the sand with one foot, then the other. It didn't make me feel any better.

Then I heard a voice: "Gabrielle!" I didn't turn around; I kept walking. Bear started running after me. I ran away from him as fast as I could, back toward the car.

"Wait up," he called, quickening his pace. "Wait!" he called louder. I ran faster toward Buffy's car, the wicker basket hitting against my leg, the wine glasses clinking against each other. His steps got closer, and the closer he got, the more I wanted to get away. My keys were ready. As I unlocked the door and opened it, his hand pushed the car door closed.

"Don't talk to me!" I screamed, trying to push his hand away. "Get away from me. Just get away." He put his hand over mine. "Don't touch me, I don't want you near me, do you hear," I said, turning to face him.

"Listen to me," he said, his teeth clenched, his body taut.

"No!" I said. "I don't want to hear anything you have to say. It's finished." The words poured out, surprising even me.

"Gabrielle, you're overreacting."

All I could do was take a few deep breaths to keep from hyperventilating. "Overreacting! Now you're going to start turning it around as if it's my fault. I came here with the best of intentions to tell you how I felt. Oh, what's the use, go back to your Sherri," I said.

Bear's expression softened. "Sherri doesn't mean anything to me, she's just a girl," he said. "That has nothing to do with us."

"That's funny, I thought it did. I guess we see things differently."

"But you didn't want to go to Santa Barbara. I asked you first."

"What did you do, recast on the freeway?"

"God, what do you expect, celibacy from a guy?"

"The only thing I expect from you is trust between us and not to be replaced in a few minutes on the freeway. Is that too much to ask?"

"I just stopped at a light on Sunset and there was Sherri. So I pulled over and we talked for a while."

"Must have been quite a conversation."

"Oh, we had a few laughs."

"I bet."

"About cars, traffic, about how one honk meant yes and two honks meant no."

154

"That's real cute," I said.

Bear had a need to explain further. "I only met her three times, once at a flower shop, then the Renaissance Fair with you, and then on the freeway when I invited her to Santa Monica."

"Is that when she honked once?" I asked. "Was she driving in the fast lane?"

He came around toward me, his tone concerned. "You're getting all upset about this," he said, trying to calm me down.

"Yes, I am. What did you have to go with her for . . . I mean, if we have something going between us, if we care about each other, why couldn't you go alone? Why did you have to bring Little Bo Peep?"

"It's no big deal," he said. "It's you I care about."

No big deal. His words reverberated in my ears. "No big deal, I see." I opened the car door. "You know, I think your attitude stinks!" I started to get into the car. "I'll be seeing you."

"Gabrielle!"

"No big deal!"

He stepped back and let me go. "Where do you think you're living?" he yelled at me, scowling.

I took another deep breath. "Everything is replaceable, isn't it? Even me!" I said passionately. He was caught by surprise. His mouth opened very slightly, but no words came out. "Boy," I said, "some things are thrown away so quickly, aren't they?"

"Maybe some things should be tossed out—if they begin to own us," he said, staring at me.

"The way I see it," I said, "you don't run off with another person if you care about someone."

"Gabrielle," he said, "stay. I'll tell her to leave." He started running his finger along my arm but now his touch turned me cold. He gave me the shivers.

"Go on back and have a few more laughs." I slipped into the front seat and slammed the door closed. As I backed the car up, he opened the car door.

"You forgot something." He handed me the wicker basket I had left outside the car.

"Thank you."

I started to drive out of the parking lot and he called after me, "When you take a few steps into the modern age, call me." I stopped the car and leaned out the window.

"Where I come from people have feelings. And if that's going out of style, then I want to stay old-fashioned."

He spoke with sudden urgency. "You haven't cornered the market on feelings, you know."

"Oh," I answered, "I'm glad you told me that. I thought you'd just hire a lawyer to deal with yours."

I stepped on the accelerator and peeled out of the driveway. He called after me, "Have a nice life." And that was the last I heard.

Bear stood there watching me until I pulled onto the road. I knew one of the wine glasses had broken, probably in all that running. The light turned green and I took one last look at the neon lights of the Miramar Hotel. A blanket of mist was rolling in from the ocean, and I thought that Room 37 could have been so cozy and nice.

Bear and Sherri played back in my mind like a bad dream. "Have a nice life." His words rang so hollow. It was almost as if we were strangers to each other. Here I'd thought we might even be spending our lives together, and he was dismissing me with, "Have a nice life." My mind felt like it was in overload—too much thinking. I turned the radio on. Cars were driving next to me on the freeway, and in a funny way, I felt more in tune with them than I did with Bear.

When I arrived home Buffy was playing Pitfall with Zack. Then she heard me calling her. "Gabrielle, is that you?" She sounded surprised.

"Yes, it's me all right," I yelled up the stairs, but Buffy was already halfway down.

"What happened?" she said. "I pictured you two at a lovely picnic on the beach."

"Yeah, well, it turned out to be a barbecue instead, and I got burned."

Zack had finished his video game and came downstairs in time to hear me retell the afternoon's events. He stood there pulling on his beard, nodding his head up and down knowingly.

When I finished, Buffy nudged Zack. "I smell the wood burning."

"Well, I was just thinking." He stroked his beard some more. "The only one you're running away from is yourself."

"What are you talking about?" I asked, starting to get really angry.

"Wake up, kid, or the world will pass you right by," he said.

"Nothing is passing me by," I answered furiously.

He smiled, " 'Exclusively Yours' should be the motto put on your T-shirt."

"That's not the point."

"What is the point?" he asked.

"Well, the point is that I shouldn't have gone. I didn't really want to go but I was so depressed and miserable. I didn't know what to do and Buffy thought that I should go. I mean, I'm not blaming her for what I did or the way it turned out. All I'm saying is, I don't think it's fair for you to force your values on me. I mean, it has to be right for me, not right for you."

Buffy was about to speak but Zack beat her to it. "Come on," he said, "if it turned out differently you wouldn't be yelling."

"What's so terrible about going away with him? You've known him for over a month," Buffy said.

"What does time have to do with it?" I asked.

"It's not like you're rushing into anything," she said.

"Well, I don't want to be pushed into anything either. You and Zack got together when you were ready. I'll get it together when I'm ready." .

Buffy and Zack were sitting next to each other on the couch, and suddenly it dawned on me that we had set up teams, Buffy and Zack on one side, me on the other. "It's like you're sitting there judging me. Like you and Zack have all the answers and you're right. Who are you to tell me, anyway."

Buffy tried to ease the tension in the air. "We took the plunge and we survived."

"So what?" I said and got up and started pacing the room. "We're not kids anymore, when we dressed alike so people would think we were identical twins."

Buffy's eyes met Zack's. A wall seemed to be building up between us.

"You know, Buffy, I thought you were my friend, my best friend. I supported you when you made your decision about the baby. The least you can do is support me now."

Buffy began to twist her hands nervously. She was actually at a loss for words.

"Why can't you respect my opinion?" I continued. "Why

158

can't you respect what I'm struggling with? I don't have to do the same as you do. I mean, if you're my friend, you'll love me and back me up like I backed you up."

Buffy was caught off-guard, and Zack had the good sense to keep out of it. He sat there silently. Then, with all the passion I felt, I added, "I mean, Buffy, friendship isn't just memories."

She didn't say anything and neither did I for a moment. Then I spoke again. "What's good for you isn't necessarily good for me. I mean, you're just as right as I am. We're just different, that's all."

Buffy stood up. She came over to me and threw her arms around me. "You're right," Buffy said. "We can change, and love each other for it. I mean, that's what we wanted all this time, isn't it?"

"Yes," I said, "yes." Then I pulled away from her. "You know what's happening to us right this very second, Buffy? We're growing up!"

Zack smiled. "Watch it, it could be contagious."

We all burst out laughing. "It certainly beats crying," I said.

"It certainly does," said Buffy. Then she turned to me, only half joking, "You're not going to pack up and go home, are you?" she asked.

"Go home!" I answered. "Are you kidding? I'm here for the summer."

During the next few days, an hour didn't pass in which I didn't think about Bear. I wondered whether he was working in the studio or swimming in his pool, or missing me even a little. In an odd way, though, the pain of not being with him didn't produce the usual anxiety. If our relationship was without a belief in each other, I thought to myself, I'd rather know it now, early on, than later, because it would only be more painful in the long run.

During this time Buffy and I spent more time together than we had since I arrived. At some level we were busily building a bridge to the next place we were going. A bridge that could hold us together for the next ten years. And then we'd have to build another one.

The only major setback I had was on Monday afternoon. The intense heat seeped through the seams of the house. No one was home except me. Buffy was out with Zack planting trees in the foothills of the Sierra Madres. They had wanted me to go, but I wasn't in the mood for smog-resistant trees that day. I had a very strong need to talk to my mother, so I went over and picked up the telephone.

"Hello, Mom," I said.

"Hi, Gabrielle, dear, how are you doing?"

"All right," I said, my voice quavering a little.

"What's the matter? You seem . . . you seem . . ."

And with that I burst into tears.

"Please, Gabrielle," she asked, over my tears, "what is it?" The frustration at being far away was obvious in her voice. All the tension poured out of me at the sound of her voice. At that moment I would have given anything for my mother to hold me in her arms and tell me everything would be better tomorrow.

"Are you okay?" Her voice sounded alarmed.

"Yes, Mom," I answered reassuringly, and I took a few short breaths to help me control my tears. "I just needed to have a good cry with you, like old times."

"Are you getting homesick?" she said. "You can come home

160

whenever you want—you don't have to wait for a special assigned day to do that, you know!" Her voice was warm and supportive. "It doesn't mean you've failed or anything if you want to come home."

I was so glad she was my mother even if she was far away. "No, Mom, I want to stay till the end of summer. I feel better now."

"I love you very much," she said into the phone.

"I love you, too," I whispered back.

"It's good to have a good cry. The world looks a lot better after you get it off your chest."

"Yes," I answered, "I'll speak to you soon and give a big hug to Daddy."

"He's outside washing the car. Wait a minute, I'll call him in."

"No, no, no, Mom," I said, stopping her, "this call was just for us. Tell him I'll call back for him tomorrow. Good-bye." And she let me hang up first, like she always did.

Suddenly I began to feel cooped up. Buffy's car was parked in the driveway and I decided to take a drive. I was hungry to see people. Even during this busy rush hour, very few people were walking in the streets. Most of them were in cars, surrounded by steel and glass. There were Chevrolets, Buicks, Porsches, Mercedes, and I counted seven Rolls-Royces. I exchanged glances with just one other person, that was because I had to see what someone looked like who had a license plate that said, "I'm God."

Before I knew it I was passing Tishman-West and making a right onto Westwood Boulevard. And there she was, sitting on the blue bench. I was glad there was some consistency in the world.

At first she didn't see me pull up to the curb. Her attention was on a lady standing on the corner and screaming at the top of her lungs. It made me think she should be singing in an opera, because she had quite a voice. People walked past her, curious at first, then breaking into laughter. It wasn't until I honked that the bag lady noticed I was there.

"Come on." I waved, without being able to predict what her reaction would be. But without a moment's hesitation, she opened the door and slipped right in, throwing her life's possessions in the backseat. She pointed with her chin to the screaming lady.

"At least I'm not crazy," she said, straightening out her dress.

"Does she come here often?"

"No, I've never seen her before in my life, but she's got some set of pipes on her." She began to rub the upholstery as if it were velvet. "Oh, I haven't been in one of these in a long time. It feels so . . . so exclusive." Just the way she phrased things made me laugh. "Where are we going?" she asked in a perky voice, with a twinkle in her eye.

"Anywhere you want."

I stepped on the gas and made a right. Slowly, I drove down Wilshire Boulevard while she pondered various possibilities. Then her eyes lit up. "Go to the corner and take a right." We turned off Wilshire Boulevard and proceeded down a few blocks. "A left here," she directed, "now a right."

After a few miles she signaled with her hand. "Another right here at the stop signal." I was totally lost, but she seemed to know exactly where we were going.

"Where are we heading?" I asked.

She simply nodded reassuringly. "You'll see any minute now. We're not on a wild goose chase, I'll tell you that."

Her foot slammed on an imaginary brake midway down the quiet residential block. "Stop here!"

"Here?" I asked. "What's here?"

"You'll see," she said, halfway out the door. "It's okay, dearie."

The white paint on the little Cape Cod house was peeling off and the green mailbox in front hung on a few hinges. We walked through a small front yard and she peeked in the window.

"What are you doing?" I asked her. "We don't want to get into trouble."

"No, no," she said. "I used to live here."

"Here?" I said, almost falling over.

"See there, that's where I kept my television set and my dishes and my husband."

"You had a husband, too?"

"That surprises you?"

"Well, yes, a little." I tried not to let on how much.

"Yeah, he drank too much, the old buzzard. He'd buy an old heap of a car and he'd get soused for a few months and forget to make the payments, so they'd come around and repossess it. That went on for eight years until they finally took away our house. The poor guy went on to greener pastures."

"Oh, no."

She peeled another piece of paint off. "Ah," she said, "being happy doesn't last forever. C'mon, dearie, cheer up. I'm better off now, believe me."

"But don't you miss your home?" I asked.

She gave the question some thought. "Well, sometimes I miss my nice soft quilt. It was all broken in and everything. But, no, I like having just my clothes and all I can carry. Anything more than that is excess baggage as far as I'm concerned."

"And your husband, don't you miss him?" I asked.

"Are you crazy? It ain't what it's cracked up to be. I like my little bench. I know that no creditor is going to pull it out from under me."

After she finished pointing out the living room with the molding that she and her husband had carved together, she felt the tour was over. "Enough of that," she said, walking back to the car. She picked a few leaves from the hedges bordering the house and slipped them in her pocket. We drove back toward Westwood, then I dropped her off across the street from her bench. "It's good to be home," she said, pulling her bags out of the backseat.

"I liked your house," I said. She seemed pleased.

"Next time I'll show you something else," she said, adjusting her dress and slamming the door closed. "I'll see you," she said.

"Wait a minute," I called. "I don't even know your name."

"Sarah," she said.

The Beverly Hills bus honked for me to get out of the way.

"Good-bye, Sarah," I said.

When I got back to the house Zack's car was in the driveway and so was the Byrons'. The smell of roast chicken and rice greeted me at the door. It felt warm and homey, and I realized I was beginning to feel comfortable here.

Mom Byrons was cutting up some cucumbers for a salad, and I picked up some radishes and started slicing them, tasting every third piece. Buffy mixed the salad dressing in an old mayonnaise jar. We all caught up on each other's day. Mr. Byrons and Zack were called for dinner, and we sat around the table and talked. Mr. Byrons told us about a group of economic purists who had come to his class at U.C.L.A. They had visited a past-life reader, who told them they were all part of a group that had manufac-

164

tured the cotton gin and that they themselves had changed our economic structure—in a former life, that is. Then Mom Byrons mentioned her new idea about selling hand-painted scarves mailed directly from the ashram.

Buffy and Zack told about some three-hundred-year-old eucalyptus trees they'd seen that day and how they'd heard that trees talk to each other in their own language. I thought to myself that if my father could be a fly on the wall, he'd be buzzing the room like a bird.

Right at that moment the bell rang. Mom Byrons seemed surprised. "Who could that be? We're not expecting anyone."

Buffy got up from the dinner table and ran to the door. When she returned, her face was pale. "Gabby, it's for you, it's Bear," she said.

Mom Byrons finished swallowing. "Why don't you show him into the den, it's quiet there." She understood.

The fork was still in my hand as I moved the rice into a heap. "Gabby, aren't you going?" Buffy said. "Aren't you going?" She urged me up.

"Yes," I said, "I'm just gathering the rice together."

When I walked into the living room, Bear was waiting for me. At first glance my heart pounded like it did when we first set eyes on each other at the carousel. That night seemed a long time ago now. And yet it was only a month since he'd thrown my heart out of whack. The attraction, the pull toward him was as strong now as it had been the moment we met.

"Hello," I said.

"Hello, Gabrielle," he said. But somehow the sound of his voice saying my name brought vividly back to me that stormy argument at the Miramar Hotel and the problems that lay unresolved between us.

"Gabrielle, I've come to apologize."

My anger and bitterness had dissipated by now.

"I'm sorry for what I said and what I did. It's taken this long for me to find the courage to ask you to forgive me. I got caught in the act and all I could do was defend myself."

"Oh." I waited for him to continue.

"I've been doing a lot of thinking about what you screamed at me the other night."

"I didn't scream."

"Please," he said. "I'm trying to apologize.

"You know," I said, "when I first met you, I was overwhelmed with all you could do and with all you had. And then I discovered much to my surprise that you were just like everyone else."

"So you finally figured me out," he said.

"Yes, you weren't that perfect prince I thought you were."

"Well, I knew that all the time," he said.

"And you treat people as if they can be just thrown away." I thought for a moment. "You know, Bear, we don't even know each other. I mean, we've been seeing each other for over a month, but our relationship has been a fraud."

"How?" he asked.

"Well, we don't really know each other, how we feel, things like that. We haven't gotten deeper than the first layer of an onion."

"Maybe," he said, "the problem is you haven't looked. Because if you'd looked you'd see I do have feelings, too." He cleared his throat. "And you know, you haven't let me see who you really are either."

"Well, I'm just beginning to find out myself."

"And what are you finding out?"

166

"I'll tell you what," I said. "I realize now that I don't have to go to bed with you or not go to bed with you for me to be grown up. It's hearing my own voice that matters." It came to me that very second like I had solved a mathematical equation. "Hearing my own voice—not yours or Buffy's or my mother's—that's how I become a woman. That's how I grow up."

Bear seemed interested in this profound discovery of mine.

I continued, "Then I don't have to worry if you like me or the world likes me because the only person that has to like me is me."

"Can I get a word in?" Bear said.

"Yes."

"Well, I do like you, I like you a lot like this. I like your conviction."

I thought about what I had just said and I wished I could make a recording of it and play it back whenever I got scared or lost track of who I was. "I've got to trust my feelings, they're all I've got," I said.

"I've never heard you speak like this before," he said.

"That's because I've never felt like this before," I said. "You see, you no longer have power over me."

"Gabrielle, I never wanted any power over you."

"But I let you have it. You know, Bear, this is really my first relationship."

He didn't seem surprised. He looked at me. "In a funny way, Gab, it is for me, too."

I laughed. "And I don't think I'm doing too well at it."

"So we're both falling a little on our faces, but who cares, maybe that's how we learn," he said, reaching out to me.

The intensity of this conversation was getting too much. "Why are relationships so hard?" I said.

Bear stood there, tall, handsome, his hands in his pockets. "My parents have been married for over twenty years, which is a record for this place, and they do time and a half, believe me."

I had to laugh. "Mine, too."

He looked right into my eyes. "Sometimes I wonder if you care about me as much as I care about you."

"Of course I do." My eyes betrayed my feelings before the words.

"Sometimes I need reassurance that we can make it."

For the first time he seemed vulnerable to me, like I could reach out and touch him, really touch him. "We can make it happen," I said, "if we want to work at it. It's up to us."

His eyes closed for a second. "I'd like that very much." And then he smiled. "But work," he gulped, "you want to put me to work?"

"Yes, I do," I said.

And he shook his head. "Then you've got yourself a job." He extended his hand to me, his expression serious. "Friends?"

"Friends," I answered. My hand gripped his. "Let's shake on it."

Our relationship was moving into a different sphere, and although I felt a great surge of love, it wasn't that the bells were ringing loudly and knocking me out. I wanted his love to warm me, not control me. And I took the power I had previously given to him, the power that made me want to please someone at my own expense, to make him believe I was something I was not, I took this power and gave it back to myself.

He pulled me to him, his arms warm and protective around me. "You make me want to be a better person, you know. That's your crime."

"I plead guilty," I said, smiling. It felt good to be in his arms. Then out of nowhere Little Bo Peep came running through my mind. At first I tried to push her out. And then I thought that in an odd way she had helped us find our way back to each other.

He looked down at me. "What are you smiling about?" he asked.

At first it seemed silly to say, but then it didn't. "Little Bo Peep lost her sheep and didn't know where to find them, leave them alone and they'll come home, wagging their tails behind them."

"You were thinking about a nursery rhyme?" He reached down to kiss me. And I stood on my tiptoes.

"Just a nursery rhyme," I said.

He held me tighter than before, and our lips released all the tension and fear of what we had almost lost, and celebrated what we had found together.

Suddenly my stomach growled, and we laughed. "All this talk is giving me an appetite." We rummaged through the kitchen, but all I could find were seeds and whole wheat pita bread. "Oh, let's go get a candy bar," I said, putting back a jar of wheat germ.

"I know the perfect place."

And in a second we were out of the house. We rode to Thrifty's Drugs and bought a month's supply of Hershey bars, Baby Ruths, Milk Duds, and Milky Ways for me to keep stashed away. "This should last for the rest of the summer," I said. Later he dropped me off at Buffy's, and we kissed each other goodnight.

"All this emotion can really exhaust a guy." He sighed.

"It's much harder than schoolwork," I had to agree.

It was silent in the house. Everyone seemed to have gone to bed, everyone, that is, except Mom Byrons. She loved to prowl the night.

"I heard you come in, dear," she said softly. "Everything all right?"

And I began to tell her all that had happened as she flipped some switches. "Plugging us into Bel Air Patrol for the night," she said.

"It's like they tuck us in," I mused.

"No, they patrol the night. *I* tuck you in."

Mom Byrons stood by the lamp, her hand on the switch, but she didn't turn it off. "Gabrielle, you came here because you wanted to be free, and somehow you were looking for it on your trip to California. But there's all kinds of space you can be free in. You can be free in your mind—that's the best place of all. Don't you see? It's all up here," she said, pointing to her head. "Freedom is a state of mind. You just have to be ready to take it. But once you've found it, you'll never want to give it up."

The words touched a deep chord within me. "You know, Mom Byrons, in a funny way, I think tonight I found a small part of it."

She turned out the light. "I think you have, too. Being happy by yourself is the first step to being free."

We said goodnight and went upstairs. I went into my room, but I was so excited, I couldn't settle down. I tiptoed downstairs and grabbed a bottle of champagne from the bar. Buffy and I had bought it one day and were saving it for a special occasion. I knew she wouldn't mind if I drank it all by myself. I got a wine glass and went back up to my room.

Out the window was the night sky. As I watched the pattern

of light and shadows against the darkness, I felt something happening inside me. I felt a part of me dying and making room for someone else, so far nearly a total stranger to me. I no longer felt afraid to be different, because, after all, being true to yourself was synonymous with daring to be different.

I took the glass of champagne in my hand. I had another toast to make. I held the glass up against the dark cool window. *"To me,"* I toasted. *"To me, Gabrielle Fuller, and to life!"*

ABOUT THE AUTHOR

Bonnie Zindel was born and raised in New York City and spent five years living in Beverly Hills, California. Of her move she writes, "We felt a tremendous culture shock coming from New York. They say that New Yorkers are the hardest converts, and I think it's true." Her other works include *A Star for the Latecomer,* a novel that she wrote with her husband, Paul Zindel, and *I Am a Zoo,* a play that was produced off-off-Broadway.

Bonnie Zindel lives in New York City with her husband and two children, David and Lizabeth.